ISBN 979-8-9897701-8-2

Published by Hidden Hand Press
www.hiddenhandbooks.com

FATHERS AND SONS

by Joshua Bartolome

CONTENTS

BARKER, ALBERTA

It wasn't supposed to happen.

Our doctor told us that Annie's due date was for December. But for whatever reason, she started having labour pains while we were on a trip to her mother's home in Calgary. Exam after exam showed that nothing was wrong with our unborn son. This is why I refuse to believe that it was merely a matter of bad luck when her water broke as we travelled down Highway 63.

Something wanted us to be there.

I floored the gas pedal and Annie shrieked like she was being gutted with a fishhook. I had never heard someone scream like that before.

To control my trembling hands, I gripped the steering wheel until my knuckles turned white while simultaneously keeping an eye out for any passing cars. I was going twenty kilometres above the speed limit, and I really didn't want to be pulled over by a roving traffic cop.

Strangely, the highway had been empty ever since we left Fort McMurray. We were at least another hour or two away from the nearest town, and no matter how hard I pushed the ailing Sedan that I had inherited from my grandfather, we would never reach a hospital in time. Using my free hand, I activated my Bluetooth earpiece and called 911.

A blast of static almost ruptured my eardrum before the flaying noise settled into a low drone. I slammed my fist against the dashboard and cursed the horrible cell phone reception. However, Annie's plaintive wailing forced me to calm down, and I attempted another call.

"911, what's your emergency?" a female operator answered after a single ring.

"My wife's giving birth," I said. "Please, I need help."

"Are you driving to a hospital right now, sir?"

"Yeah, but we're pretty far. I'm not sure we'll make it."

"Did your wife's water break?"

"She's bleeding."

"Stay on the line, okay? I'm tracking your signal and it looks like you're close to a clinic."

"Where?"

"It's in the town of Barker. You'll have to keep going another three kilometres."

I was flabbergasted.What the hell was she talking about?

"Lady, there aren't any towns between Fort Mac and Breynat. Are you sure about this?"

"Sir, I know you're worried, but I need you to trust me. If you follow my instructions, I can guarantee that your wife will have all the medical assistance required for a safe delivery."

I wanted to say something else, but the operator's self-assured tone stifled the sense of unease that was unfurling within my stomach like a grotesque vine. As far as I could remember, there were no municipalities along this isolated highway flanked by thick woodland.

"You'd better be right," I grumbled.

The smell of blood filled the Sedan's interior, and the taste of copper lingered on my tongue. Annie's cries had dwindled into a low, constant moaning, while a puddle of red liquid began to form on the black rubber mats beneath her shoes.

Jesus, I thought. *Help me. Please.*

I kept on driving for what seemed like half an hour. Still, there were no towns in sight. The car's headlights sliced through the thick evening gloom, revealing nothing but an endless stretch of asphalt bisected by a yellow fluorescent line.

"Am I close?" I asked the operator.

"Five minutes away."

Then, as if on cue, a green, pockmarked metal sign came into view, standing by the highway. Behind it, an unpaved gravel road wound through a field of ripe barley stalks that swayed like a living carpet as a cool breeze blew across. The post's faded, white letters read:

BARKER, ALBERTA

POPULATION – 50

In the distance, just beyond the field, loomed silhouettes of houses and other small establishments that clustered together in a tight-knit huddle. Right then, I remembered a joke my father used to tell about a homeless man who saw a giraffe in a zoo for the very first time and declared, with a lunatic's iron-clad self-confidence, that "there ain't no such animal."

I grew up in this province.

I've crossed this highway more times than I could count.

There ain't no such town, I thought, disbelieving.

Not around here.

***

While driving through Barker's main avenue, I noticed that all the windows of every establishment were devoid of all light and movement, and aside from the faint, orange glow of street lamps, there were no other sources of illumination in this desolate village.

By this time, Annie had ceased making any sounds altogether. Beads of sweat slid down her pallid skin. Nonetheless, I could tell by her agonised expression that my wife was still in pain, although she could scarcely manage a single, weakened whimper.

Despite our dire circumstances, I still couldn't rid myself of that insistent, nagging feeling that something was very, very wrong with our surroundings. We had already passed two dry goods retailers, a hardware shop, a consignment store, a small grocery, and a quaint family dinner, the kind that usually served hashbrowns and eggs over-easy for breakfast.

All of these places were empty, with no townsfolk in sight.

"Where is everyone?" I muttered.

No other vehicles drove down the road. No people strolled along the pavements. At 6:15 in the evening, even the smallest, backwater towns in rural Alberta weren't as deserted as this.

"Sir, you need to focus," the operator piped up. "Do you see a rotunda ahead?"

"Yeah."

"Keep going north. You'll see the clinic on the right."

Pressing down hard on the gas, I catapulted the Sedan toward the town's central landmark. Our car fishtailed along the marble rotunda's edge, and for a brief second, I caught an intricately sculpted brass mastiff standing atop a granite pedestal, its fangs bared in an eternal, frozen snarl.

At that moment, the statue didn't seem too strange, since my thoughts were preoccupied with the survival of Annie and our son. Things are much different now. The more I think about that sculpture, the more I feel as if its eyes had been watching us, like a wolf stalking a pair of rabbits.

Soon enough, to my relief, I saw a bright red neon emergency sign flashing like a lighthouse beacon in the midst of a storm. The sign's crimson glare bled across the parking lot housing only a pair of ambulances that looked as though they came straight from the 1970's.

"Baby, just hold on," I whispered to Annie while parking the car outside of Barker Community Hospital. She merely nodded, eyes half-closed, before slipping into unconsciousness.

Silently, I prayed to God and whoever was watching in heaven that we weren't too late.

"Help!" I screamed while running to the main entrance. "Someone, please! Help us!"

I rushed through the front doors, charging without breaking stride, and only stopped to catch my breath upon reaching the emergency triage area. All the lights were on. Clipboards and pens and charts lay in neatly-ordered rows across the reception desk, but I couldn't find any doctors or paramedics or medical staff anywhere. The place was completely, utterly empty.

"Hello?" I shouted. "My wife's dying, for God's sake!"

No one answered.

Only the dull thrum of ventilators could be heard throughout the ward.

"Sir?" the operator's voice buzzed in my earpiece. "What's going on?"

"There's no one here!"

"Maybe it's a slow night. There should be at least two nurses on duty."

"What do you think I am, stupid? I'm telling you, there isn't anyone in this place!"

I wanted to give up. Fear and desperation washed over me in nauseating waves. The thought of losing both Annie and our baby boy in this godforsaken town was too much to bear.

"Don't lose your head, Martin," the operator said.

"What did you just call me?"

"Your name," she replied. "I heard your wife saying it while you were driving. Take a deep breath and calm down, because you can't help her if you start panicking."

Yes, the operator was right. I had to stay focused – for Annie's sake.

"I'm sending over an ambulance," she continued. "They'll be driving all the way from Fort Mac, but they should arrive in about an hour, okay? Until then, we have to do what we can."

"Are you shitting me?"

"Martin, your wife is losing a lot of blood. I know you're scared, but we won't get anywhere if we don't work together. You have to do your part, all right?"

"Okay, okay. Tell me what to do."

"Find a wheelchair. We need to get her inside."

***

Annie was barely breathing when I returned to our car.

"No, no, no," I said. "Please, don't do this."

Her skin was pale, dotted with cold beads of sweat. She drew in short gasps of breath like a fish suffocating on dry land. "Stay with me, baby," I begged while lifting her onto the wheelchair.

Blood had been dripping from between Annie's legs and had left a glistening trail as I wheeled her into the emergency ward, staining the hospital's bizarrely spotless, lime-green linoleum.

"Martin, save our boy," she said weakly. "Please."

"I'll save you both."

Annie gave me this tired, sorrowful gaze while I pushed the wheelchair into the nearest surgical area I could find. The overhead lights in the operating room had been left on. Operating tools lay inside nearby medical overbed tables. Scalpels, forceps, and other sharp implements twinkled with a sinister gleam beneath the bright sterile glow of fluorescent bulbs.

"Promise me," Annie said, her words barely audible.

How could I say no when she looked at me with those eyes?

"I will," I replied. "I promise."

Just then, the operator spoke through my earpiece.

"Martin? Are you there?"

"Yeah."

"I need you to help your wife lie down on the bed."

"She won't stop bleeding."

"We'll try to stop it. Hurry."

I gently tapped Annie's face to rouse her.

"Baby?" I said. "I'm gonna lift you up, okay?"

She didn't answer.

"Annie?"

Trembling, I placed my index finger beneath her nose. I couldn't feel air being exhaled.

"Annie?!"

My hands next went to the side of her neck.

No pulse.

"Oh God," I shouted. "Oh, Jesus, Annie! Wake up!"

"Martin, talk to me," the operator said. "What's happening?"

"She isn't breathing. I can't feel a pulse."

"Try again. Blood loss slows down a person's heartbeat. It can be hard to spot."

This time, I touched Annie's wrist.

Like before, I struggled to feel even a single, subtle tremor. Sobbing, I then shook Annie vigorously, but she wouldn't respond, not even when I slapped her twice on the cheek.

"Baby, don't do this, don't leave me," I cried.

There was no use denying reality as it unfurled before my very eyes.

"Annie…my wife…she's dead," I whispered into the Bluetooth earpiece.

Whoever this bitch was—the one sitting behind that phone, nameless, faceless, and beyond my reach—I wanted to strangle her, to butcher her, to hack her body into pieces.

"I'm sorry," the operator said.

There seemed to be remorse in her words, but that didn't matter. I was beyond consoling.

"Fuck you. You're sorry? If you hadn't sent us here, my wife would still be alive!"

I slumped to the floor, weeping, and begged God and all the devils in hell to end my life, because I couldn't bear the pain any longer. Better oblivion than this.

"Look, I know you're upset, but if you don't hurry up, your son will die," the operator replied. "It takes ten minutes before the baby suffocates due to lack of oxygen."

"What the hell are you talking about?"

"Do you want your child to live?"

At first, I didn't understand what she was implying, until I caught another glimpse of the surgical tools lying side-by-side, undisturbed, within separate metal trays.

"No," I shook my head. "No fucking way!"

"You have nine minutes and thirty seconds left."

"I am not cutting my wife!"

"She begged you. You promised."

"Jesus Christ, do you understand what you're asking from me? I'm not a surgeon! I can't!"

"That's why I'm here. I'll guide you. You have the right tools lying around, correct?"

I didn't want to admit it, but she was right.

I had already failed my wife. I didn't want to fail her again.

"Follow my instructions, and your son will live," the operator continued. "Don't, and you'll lose him, too. Time's running out, Martin. You have eight minutes left."

I closed my eyes for a second.

"God fucking dammit," I said. "What should I do?"

***

"Are you ready?" the operator asked.

I gritted my teeth and began the process of carving my son out of his mother's womb. First, I set my wife gently onto the operating table, her blood spilling all over my chest. Afterwards, I used a pair of surgical scissors to cut away Annie's blouse, exposing her swollen belly.

For a second, I saw her belly rise as our baby reacted to the stimulus and kicked hard.

Seeing this almost made me weep in relief.

He was still alive.

Our son was alive.

Grabbing a scalpel, I gathered the last vestiges of willpower left in my soul, and did the unthinkable. I will not, and I cannot describe what happened during those eight minutes. The sounds, sights, and smell of that room will never leave me until the day I die. Like a clumsy, maniacal butcher, I followed the operator's instructions and desecrated my wife's corpse.

I don't know how I managed to perform a C-section on my wife without throwing up or breaking down. There are moments in a man's life where he is forced to do what is necessary, no matter how degrading it is, or violent. Some men fold and crumble, others soldier on. A man can never know the measure of his worth until he's compelled to do terrible things against his will.

When at last I managed to pull my newborn son out of my wife's womb, a monstrous joy filled my heart. Yes, my Annie was dead, but at least, at the very least, my son had survived. He bawled, and screamed, and cried furiously as if he were outraged by the obscenity I had perpetrated.

I continued to follow the operator's instructions, snipping off the umbilical cord and then swaddling my son in a blanket before placing him in a nearby incubator.

"You did well," the operator said.

I didn't have any strength left to answer. Instead, I sat down, tired beyond words.

"The ambulance will be coming soon," the operator went on. "You should get some rest."

"What do I tell them?"

Annie's blood had soaked my clothes through. How could I explain to anyone what I had just done? If the paramedics saw my wife, surely they would think I was the one who had murdered her.

"They'll understand," the operator consoled me. "You did what you had to do. You saved your child's life. Now, it's my turn to help. Leave everything to me."

"I can't sleep. Not here."

"Shhh. Close your eyes. We'll take care of your son."

Although I wanted to stay awake, a dreadful sense of fatigue overcame my body.

Leaning back against the wall, I found my eyes fluttering as I drifted toward unconsciousness. Before succumbing to a deep, dreamless sleep, I glanced at the incubator where my son lay, still crying, wailing, begging for his mother's gentle hands.

"Michael," I whispered. "His name is Michael."

I don't know how long I had been sleeping, but when I finally opened my eyes, the entire operating room was dark. Only the dull glow of red emergency lights filtered into the area.

Looking at my watch, I thought at first that it was still 6:15 p.m., but after tapping its glass surface, I soon realised that it had stopped. What had happened while I was asleep?

Where was my son?

Sheer panic flooded my veins like battery acid as I glanced around the dimly-lit operating room, searching for the incubator that housed my frail, vulnerable little boy. It wasn't there. When I glanced at the operating bed, I saw that my wife's body was also missing.

I couldn't hear Michael's plaintive screeching. I tried to calm myself down by thinking that, perhaps, the paramedics had taken him. But if that were indeed the case, then why did they leave me here? They should've woken me up, questioned me about Annie and the horrible things I had to do just to save Michael from drowning in the amniotic fluid of his mother's womb.

The operator had promised to take care of everything.

What was going on?

"Michael?" I screamed while hobbling out of the operating room, a pounding headache jackhammering my skull. I didn't know what else to do. He was barely an hour old, and he would never recognize my voice even if I shouted myself hoarse. But I had to do something to keep myself from sliding into a lunacy, and saying Michael's name in the darkness of that accursed hospital felt like intoning a prayer against the shapeless things that slithered in the shadows.

"Michael, where are you?"

Please, I thought, you've already taken too much from me. Not this one. Not my son.

Then, as if reading my mind, a familiar voice blared through the overhead speakers. In that instant, I knew, beyond certainty, that we had been led to the town of Barker for a purpose.

They wanted my child. They wanted Michael.

"He's safe," the operator's soothing voice said. "We would never harm your son. He is precious to us. It has been so long since we have welcomed a new member of our family."

Hearing those words sent a current of terror through every nerve and fibre of my being.

My legs trembled with each step, and yet I kept on walking, pressing forward, exploring the corridors, searching for a sign that could show me where they had taken Michael.

"I'll do anything," I cried out. "Just give him back."

"What exactly can you offer us, Martin?" the operator replied. "You've already served your purpose. There is nothing good and pure left in you, nothing that we can use."

I spotted a trail of blood leading into another hospital wing. The blood slithered past a closed set of double doors with two red emergency lights shining above them.

"Leave now, or die," the operator warned. "Do not return to this town, or we shall flay your soul and show you sights that will make the sun grow black with horror."

"He's my son! You have no right!"

"Do not scorn our mercy, little human, worthless piece of flesh." The operator's tone suddenly transformed, becoming a chorus of voices that belonged to thousands of people, men and women, young and old, all talking simultaneously. "We chose to spare your life because you brought this blessed child to us," the voices continued. "Our patience grows thin."

"Screw your mercy."

I wasn't the kind of guy who would shirk from a scrap – even the ones that I knew I would lose. Growing up as the only Filipino kid in a farming community in rural Alberta, I was hardened by daily fistfights with the local redneck scumbags at my high school. Life around these parts was a constant battle against everything – the weather, its people, your own self.

This fight wasn't any different. I risked losing everything. My life. My own soul. But this was a risk I was willing to take. For Michael. I would do anything and everything for him.

I had already proven that.

Blood pounded in my ears as I pushed the double doors open and walked into what seemed to be a morgue whose walls were caked with a veiny, rust-like substance that pulsated hideously. Dozens of black body bags lay on steel gurneys that flanked the dimly-lit hallway. Some of these containers squirmed like vinyl cocoons that contained larvae of monstrous proportions.

I didn't have the energy, curiosity or the madness to unzip these things and look inside.

My senses had gone numb by this time. Not even the bizarre squelching noises coming from the closed room at the end of the hall was enough to dissuade me from approaching.

What on earth was going on inside?

The closer I came, the more sounds seemed to emanate from behind the next set of double doors. White light filtered through two semi-transparent glass windows.

Through these windows, I could see shadowy, indistinct figures darting about.

The closer I came, the more sounds seemed to emanate from behind the next set of double doors. White light filtered through two semi-transparent glass windows. Through them, I could see shadowy, indistinct figures darting about.

A buzzing filled my head, like insect wings vibrating at a rapid speed and high frequency. The shrill noise was enough to bring me to my knees.

I thought the blood vessels inside my ears would burst.

When the unnatural din subsided, I rose to my feet and stumbled onward to the morgue where I thought that Michael was being held captive but I was wrong. He wasn't there.

But I did see things in that room – indescribable things, faceless things that looked like naked, sexless, human beings with the semi-translucent wings of cicadas. They had no eyes, or ears, only mouths lined with blackened, rotting teeth. In the centre of the room, lying on an autopsy table, was the almost unrecognisable body of my wife, the only woman I had ever loved.

And they were eating her.

***

I ran.

Like a coward.

There is only so much horror that the human consciousness can process before its flame dies, snuffed by the cold, bony fingers of fear. Callous laughter followed as I ran out of the hospital and jumped into the sedan. I screamed hysterically when I started the car and drove away.

I kept on going, past the rotunda with its statue of the snarling dog, past the abandoned shops, houses, and buildings that flanked the road into Barker. I did not stop until I made it all the way to the township of Breynat. What happened in the days that followed cannot compare to the horrors which I had witnessed, but it would not be an overstatement to say that my life was ruined, forever.

I will not go into detail about the legal proceedings that have hounded me ever since I escaped with my sanity barely intact. But I have to make it known that I didn't abandon my son nor my wife.

I tried to go back to that cursed place. I even brought a constable from the Boyle RCMP detachment to accompany me, since I didn't dare return to Barker, not without a gun. When we arrived at the spot where Barker's metal signpost once stood, the bewildered police officer found nothing but trees and a field of uncut barley. At the risk of looking like a madman, I insisted that this town actually existed, that I had driven along its streets, smelled the petrichor rising from the rain-kissed asphalt, but he wouldn't believe me

We drove along that empty stretch of highway until we ended up in the outskirts of Fort McMurray. Then we turned around and travelled to Breynat again, and during those two trips, we saw no houses, no buildings, no shops, not even a dirt road that might lead back to Barker.

It had all vanished, completely, into thin air. It was as if nothing had happened.

In the end, I was handcuffed, thrown in jail, and indicted for the murder of my wife and son. The blood on my shirt, which tested positive for Annie's DNA, was used as evidence against me. Nonetheless, during the lengthy trial that attracted the attention of both local and foreign media, I didn't change my story—that a town called Barker took my family away.

The female lawyer who handled my case, in a brilliant but utterly dishonest move, claimed insanity as a legal defence, something which I had vehemently opposed.

Why should I lie to save myself from jail? I have already gone through hell, I have seen what it looks like, and there is nothing that any esteemed courts of human justice can do that would be worse than seeing my dead wife being devoured by demons. Through some stroke of devilish misfortune, the jury accepted this defence. They declared me innocent by reason of insanity.

After five years inside a psychiatric institution in Ponoka, I was set free due to good behaviour. Annie's grieving family protested my release, but by this point, the damage was already irreversible. I didn't have the time to dwell on the mistakes of the past or on broken relationships.

I had a job to do.

Ever since my release, I've been travelling all across North America and Europe, searching for information about mysterious towns that have appeared and vanished without explanation.

This has led me to the hidden corners of the world, seeking forbidden answers and finding very few. But I keep on searching anyway, and I believe that my journey is almost finished. I wasn't the first person to have experienced this sort of bizarre phenomenon. Far from it.

Throughout human history, men, women and children have strayed into towns like Barker. The earliest reports of such places can be found in the "Unaussprechlichen Kulten" written by Friedrich von Junst in 1839. In it, he described malignant creatures known as the "Feldgeister," the field spirits, or faeries in English, Irish, and Germanic mythology.

These things are not the tiny, friendly beings often seen in Disney movies. They are a malevolent, uncanny, and ancient race who have lived for centuries in the hollow, forgotten places of the earth, where old blood was spilled on old soil. They cannot reproduce like other creatures, and the only way they can continue their lineage is by transforming infants and young children—children like my son.

I believe that the thing that led us there, the creature that impersonated a 911 operator, was a faerie that von Junst called "Die Roggenmutter," the Rye Mother, the oldest and most dangerous of its kind. I don't know what sorts of monstrous things they've done to Michael, but I swear that I will, somehow, find a way to undo her dark magic. There has to be a way.

And so, armed with my hard-won knowledge and a sawed-off shotgun loaded with blessed silver buckshot, I travel down the lonely roads of America, searching for a place that exists beyond space and time. I've traded my grandfather's sedan for a black V-8 Interceptor, something that can go fast and hard and has the roar of an enraged beast chasing after its helpless, frightened prey.

I'm no longer the coward that ran away like a little child. The Feldgeister have robbed all hope, and joy, and goodness from my soul and left nothing but a seething fury.

I will bring fire and death and violence to the town of Barker. I will burn down its buildings until nothing remains but a smouldering field of ash and cinders. When that time comes, I will take back from those sons of bitches the dignity and the love they had stolen from me.

And then I will see my little boy again.

Wait for me, Michael.

I'm coming for you.

ASWANG

"I've heard that you can buy anything in Manila," Jimmy Kellow said while watching the nauseating array of nightclub lights that flickered outside the taxi's windows. "Is that true?"

He watched as the Filipino driver tightened his grip on the steering wheel. The man looked like all the other losers Jimmy had met during his travels, these poor bastards, eyes sunken from lack of sleep, brows furrowed, bodies slouched forward in the eternal posture of defeat.

"What do you have in mind?" the driver asked.

"I'm thinking of dinner, but I don't wanna do it alone."

"I know a place," the driver said. "There's a hotel called the Mariposa nearby. The price is cheap, and the service is great," he paused. "Lots of pretty girls too."

"How young?"

The driver blinked.

"Young enough."

"Clean?"

"I wouldn't suggest it if they weren't."

Jimmy watched the driver's reflection in the rear-view mirror. Filipinos were notoriously shifty. They would smile, call you boss, or sir, or other honorifics reserved for knights and military officials, but you still couldn't tell what they were thinking.

Nice folk, nicer than the Thais, that was for sure, but too smart for their own good.

"You're being awfully quiet, buddy," Jimmy said, trying to break the tension. "I know you're only trying to earn a living, so I can understand if you don't wanna go through this."

"Doesn't matter what I want," the driver replied. "I'm the driver, you're the customer."

Jimmy leaned forward.

"What are you willing to do for five thousand dollars?"

"That's a lot of money."

"You haven't answered my question."

"Like I said. Anything."

"What if I need you to help me kill someone?"

The driver laughed and glanced at Jimmy through the rear-view mirror, and for the first time, their eyes met. The Filipino's face turned a shade paler, and he quickly averted his gaze.

"I don't know if I can do that."

"You're not gonna do the killing. I just need you to find a girl."

"Why?"

"I'm hungry," Jimmy said. "That's why."

Before the driver could reply, Jimmy reached into his coat pocket and pulled out a Glock 9mm. Its smooth black exterior gleamed beneath the orange light of streetlamps filtering through the windows. The driver's eyes grew wide upon seeing it.

"Don't worry. I'm still gonna pay you," Jimmy said. "I think money's a better motivator than violence, anyway. We could both benefit from this arrangement."

"Sure."

"I'm gonna ask you again. Do you want five thousand dollars, or not?"

The driver thought for a moment.

"Do I have a choice?"

Jimmy slipped the gun back into his coat.

"Smart man. I'm glad that we came to an understanding."

***

"The Mariposa," Jimmy said. "How far away is it?"

"Twenty minutes," the driver replied. "If the traffic's good, we can get there in fifteen."

"As long as we get there."

In spite of the air-conditioner blowing at full blast, beads of sweat trickled from the driver's temple. Jimmy found it fascinating, the tics and mannerisms that signified fear. He observed the driver like an entomologist watching an insect beneath the pitiless gaze of a microscope.

"What's your name?" Jimmy asked.

"My name?"

"I'd like to know who I'm doing business with," Jimmy replied. "In case I come back."

"I'm only doing this once. No more."

"That's what they all say. But I know what it's like, living in a country like this. You wake up, every single day, wondering how you're gonna feed your family. So, as the man who's offering you a way out of this mess. I think I'm entitled to know your name."

"Rogelio. My name's Rogelio."

"Do you have any children?"

"I have a daughter."

"So do I," Jimmy said. "I have a wife and two kids. Boy and a girl. I'll do anything to keep them safe. What about you? You'll do anything to protect your family, won't you?"

"Of course."

"But what if you're the one who wants to hurt them?"

"What do you mean?"

"You'll see. Just keep on driving."

***

Rogelio's lack of enthusiasm began to annoy Jimmy.

He couldn't understand why this man refused to be grateful for the opportunity that was being presented before him. Sure, Jimmy had asked for his help to commit cold-blooded murder, but in a city where a man could end up dead in a ditch for no reason, wrapped up in masking tape like a demented Christmas present, surely another dead whore was no big deal.

Perhaps Rogelio just couldn't understand what was at stake. That, Jimmy thought, could be dangerous. After all, he wasn't doing this for shits and giggles. He was doing this for his family.

"I'm not a bad person," Jimmy said.

"No. You're just a tourist. Like everyone else."

"I have a condition. I've been fighting it all my life. The best doctors money can buy have all examined me, and they don't know if my sickness is biological or psychological in nature. They call this disease hematophagy. But really, that's just another fancy word for vampirism."

"You drink... blood?"

"More specifically human blood. Only human blood," Jimmy replied. "Before you ask, no, I'm not one of those movie vampires that bursts into flames when exposed to crucifixes or sunlight. I sleep in a regular bed, not in a coffin filled with dirt, and I've been raised as a Catholic ever since I was a little boy."

Jimmy laughed at the thought.

"Funny," he continued, "in church, it's considered a sacrament to drink the blood of Christ. When you think about it, Christianity is a vampiric religion. We consume the flesh and blood of the Messiah, and by doing so, are reborn under the loving gaze of God."

"I don't understand," Rogelio said.

"Me neither, and I've been living with this ever since I was a child. At first, it was just a thirst, a terrible, terrible thirst that would keep me awake at night, wondering what the hell was wrong with me. Then, one day, while I was riding the school bus home, one of my classmates had a nosebleed. Some of the blood dripped onto the seat beside me, and in that moment, I knew exactly what I needed to slake my thirst. When everyone else had left, I bent over and licked the spots of blood congealing on the leather. Licked them all up like strawberry syrup from a spoon."

"Does your family know about this?"

"Back home, I'm just dear old dad," Jimmy replied.

He clasped his hands together.

"Sometimes, late at night, I'd find myself standing in my daughter's room, watching her sleep. Horrible thoughts would come into my head. I'd... imagine... what *her* blood would taste like. How it would stream down her neck in thick rivulets. I'd imagine myself feeding... on her."

Breathing slowly, Jimmy lapsed into silence; he felt his blood quickening, excited by the flood of images that flashed before his mind's eye: his daughter, Katie, sleeping alone, bundled up in her teddy bear-patterned down comforter, snoring softly, mouth half-opened beneath the gentle light of a nearby night lamp. Him, standing above her, a kitchen knife brandished in his left hand, his eyes glazed, reddened, tears falling down his cheeks. Then, blood – blood spurting out of Katie's severed jugular, a geyser of crimson painting the blue, pony-themed walls of her room.

"Now do you understand?" Jimmy asked. "I'm not doing this for myself. I'm doing this for my family. I'm just like you, Rogelio. I'm a father too. Wouldn't you do the same thing?"

"I'm not like you," Rogelio replied.

"You think you're better than me?"

"I think I'd have the decency to do something else."

"Oh yeah? Like what?"

"I'd take that gun and blow my brains out."

***

Frowning, Jimmy glanced at his wristwatch.

They had been going around the city for almost an hour, and he was growing impatient with every passing minute. It was 9:30 PM, and the longer he was delayed, the hungrier Jimmy got.

This hunger, however, did not come from the pit of his stomach, but from somewhere deeper, darker.

"How close are we?" Jimmy asked.

"About five more minutes."

"Yeah, you said that half an hour ago."

"If we hadn't gotten stuck in traffic, we'd be at the Mariposa already."

Jimmy gave an exasperated sigh.

"I want you to listen carefully, alright? This is what we're gonna do."

Rogelio nodded but didn't speak.

"After we find a girl at the hotel, we need to bring her back to the taxi," Jimmy continued. "I want you to drive around, look for any places where we can't be seen. I'm gonna rough her up until she's unconscious. When that's finished, I suggest that you step out of the car."

"Where am I supposed to take the body once you're done?

"Figure it out," Jimmy replied. "You know this city better than me."

"This is bullshit," Rogelio muttered.

"What did you say?"

Rogelio stared back through the rear-view mirror. There was a coldness in the driver's eyes, an emptiness that Jimmy had never seen, not even when he looked at his own reflection.

"What do you think's gonna happen if I get caught with a dead hooker in my trunk?" Rogelio went on. "In case you don't know, the cops around here don't believe in taking murderers to court. They're gonna kill me. Not you. You have an American passport. You'll get a fair trial and an expensive lawyer to bail your ass out of Muntinlupa. I got nothing but my licence."

"So?"

"I'm risking my life for you here, boss," Rogelio replied. "Five thousand isn't enough."

Jimmy took his gun out.

"You're in no position to negotiate."

Rogelio just laughed at his face.

"Oh yeah? *Putang ina, ano'ng gagawin mo?* What are you gonna do? Shoot me? Then what? You're gonna look for another loser, another taxi driver who's willing to help you kill an innocent girl? *Punyeta.* Don't kid yourself. Chances are, that driver's gonna take you straight to jail, or worse. He's gonna snatch your money, stab you, then leave you bleeding to death beside some rat-infested dumpster in Cubao. Is that what you want?"

Jimmy lowered his gun. He remembered where he was. Not in the sunny beaches of Pattaya or beneath the bright neon haze of Tokyo's sprawling skyline. This was Manila. A man's life was cheaper than a dime bag of meth in this city. Rogelio wasn't bluffing – he was fortunate to find someone willing to accompany him. He doubted his chances of finding another one again.

"You're a long way from your nice little house in the suburbs," Rogelio spoke. "If you kill me, what do you think the people out there will do? They won't give a shit how much money you have. They won't give a shit that you're white. By the time they're done with you – I swear, there won't be enough pieces of your body to scrape off the asphalt for a decent funeral back home."

Jimmy went silent for a moment, then said:

"How do I know you're not gonna report me to the cops?"

"I do what the customer wants. For a price."

"Ten thousand."

"No."

"Eleven?"

"How much do you have right now?"

"That's none of your business."

"Suit yourself."

Rogelio stepped on the gas pedal and turned the wheel. The taxi made a sharp screeching noise as it swerved towards the sidewalk. Jimmy felt the seatbelt dig into his chest when he lurched forward. "Son of a bitch," he cursed. The car stopped with a jolt outside a karaoke bar. The warbling voices of drunk patrons filtered out of the place as they attempted to sing Frank Sinatra's *My Way*.

"You have three choices," Rogelio said. "You can shoot me and get killed by the bastards inside that bar. Or you can leave my car, and we'll forget about what happened tonight."

"What's the third choice?"

"That depends on how hungry you are."

"Very."

"Food's expensive nowadays. You gotta pay if you wanna eat."

Jimmy considered his options.

"Fifteen thousand. How's that sound?"

"Good enough."

Jimmy glared at the driver.

"This better be worth it."

Rogelio turned the key and started the engine.

"It will be."

***

"Say, boss," Rogelio asked. "You know what you remind me of?"

"What?"

"An *aswang.*"

"What the hell is that?"

"When I was a little boy," Rogelio began, "my grandfather used to tell me stories about a creature that drank human blood and ate human flesh. He called it the *aswang.* A ghoul. During the day, these things live among us as normal people, but when night comes, they grow wings and fly off in search of prey. Their favourite meals are human babies – the younger, the better. For them, a foetus is like expensive caviar. If an *aswang* smells a pregnant woman sleeping while flying in the evening sky, it'll crouch on the rooftop of her home, then slip its pointed, straw-like tongue through a hole until it slithers down and pierces the woman's belly. Then, it'll suck out her baby's soft flesh and unformed bones, until the mother and the child are both dead."

"Christ," Jimmy said. "Why are you telling me this shit?"

"I'm just surprised," Rogelio said. "I've always thought that the *aswangs* were a myth. A story told to frighten children at bedtime. I never thought I'd meet one in real life."

***

"Is this it?" Jimmy asked.

Contrary to what Rogelio had claimed, the Mariposa Hotel stood in a seedy corner of Pasay City, beside a decrepit movie house whose pockmarked brutalist façade boasted crude, hand-painted posters of B-Grade horror films with ridiculous titles such as "Mecha-Shark Versus Mega Sharktopus," and "The Human Millipede: Section 20."

A row of plywood stalls manned by hawkish vendors lined the sweltering sidewalk, their voices rising like a chorus of damned souls as they peddled pirated DVDs, bootleg Louis Vuitton handbags, dried mackerel, and myrtle clusters of baby bok-choy.

"What did you expect?" Rogelio replied. "The Shangri-La?"

Jimmy had half a mind to put a bullet through the uppity little scumbag's head. In all his years of trawling the hotels and bars and beaches of Asia for the nectarine-flavoured blood of young and desperate women, no other person had talked to him in such a disrespectful manner. Jimmy was no idiot – he knew, of course, that the shithead duped him – but what choice did he have? This was Rogelio's neighborhood, and to step out into the streets of Manila would be suicide.

There was nobody he could trust. Not around here.

Better the devil you know.

"Fine," Jimmy said. "Lead the way."

***

A foetid odour seeped out of the cream-coloured walls of the Mariposa's first-floor lobby, the stench of mould and mildew and something rank and sour that Jimmy didn't recognize. The yellow light of tungsten bulbs gave the entire hall the appearance of a crime scene in an Italian Giallo film. Standing behind the front desk was a skeletal-looking clerk whose fish-like eyes had been ravaged with ophthalmoparesis, a sure sign of Korsakoff's Dementia.

"Wait here," Rogelio said, pointing at the ratty red leather lounge chairs. Jimmy, unsure of what to do, watched as the taxi driver approached the desk clerk with a friendly grin. The fish-eyed man tilted his head in a timid gesture of acknowledgment.

Although Jimmy tried to eavesdrop on their hushed conversation, he could only pick out a few of the Tagalog phrases that Rogelio spoke. Something about a room on the fourth floor, where a girl named "Jenny" waited. Throughout this one-sided dialogue, the fish-eyed man nodded in assent, his face a sombre mask that betrayed no thought or emotion. The freak then handed a key with a tag numbered "415" attached to its chain to Rogelio.

"Let's go," Rogelio called out. Jimmy reached into his coat, touched the warm alloy skin of the Glock 9mm tucked beneath his armpit as if it were an amulet against misfortune.

Then, he followed Rogelio towards the waiting elevator doors.

Upon exiting the elevator and entering the desolate fourth-floor hallway, Jimmy pulled out the handgun and held it close to his waist; nozzle pointed upwards. Rogelio gave him a smile.

"There's no need for that, boss."

"Just making sure you stick to your end of the bargain."

"Hey, I always deliver," Rogelio shrugged. "No problem."

"So you say."

"After all we've been through, you still don't trust me?"

"I'll trust you when we get the girl.

Jimmy followed Rogelio down the concourse. For a den of cheap, very possibly diseased prostitutes, the Mariposa was strangely quiet. Jimmy could hear no muted sounds of moaning and groaning, the sordid noises that accompanied illicit sex.

An oppressive silence dominated the corridor. It felt as if he were walking through a mortuary, with the sharp staccato of his footsteps as the only sound that broke the intolerable noiselessness. Jimmy's eyes darted around, throwing glances at the other closed rooms; he expected something to jump out, a nameless creature with jagged teeth and crimson-stained claws that could rake through his flesh and tear him into strips of bloody meat.

This was wrong. This was all so very wrong.

Every nerve and fibre in his body screamed for him to run as far away as possible from this place. Yet the feeling of panic was soon replaced by the awful, gnawing hunger that throbbed in the pit of his stomach. He had not tasted blood for two years of painful waiting and planning, and he couldn't afford to turn around, take a plane back to Chicago, and bring this starving monstrosity back home where his wife, son, and daughter waited for him patiently, lovingly.

He had to feed. For the sake of his family, he had to feed.

Finally, they arrived in front of room 415. Rogelio took the key out of his pocket and presented it to Jimmy; frowning, Jimmy raised the gun, pointing it at Rogelio's face.

"You first."

"All right," Rogelio replied. He inserted the key into the doorknob's hole and unlocked it. The hinges gave a groaning sound as the door to room 415 swung open, revealing the interior.

"What the hell?" Jimmy said. "What is this shit?"

There was no girl. There were only men, five of them, wearing surgical gowns and latex gloves, gathered around a gurney with immaculately white sheets that seemed to glow beneath the glare of the LED bulbs. Thick sheets of transparent plastic covered the walls, the floor, and the ceiling itself. The entire scene looked so bizarre that Jimmy couldn't suppress an amused smile.

This was a joke.

It had to be a sick, twisted joke.

Some of the surgeons – Jimmy didn't know what else to call them – sat on a plastic-covered sofa, reading tabloid newspapers or watching cat YouTube videos on their smartphones. It was as if they had been waiting for hours for someone to arrive.

Waiting for him.

A jolt of electricity blossomed across Jimmy's ribs, flooding his body with an agony so stark, so blinding, he couldn't even let out a single, pathetic whimper. At first, as he convulsed on the corridor's grimy linoleum, Jimmy thought that he was having a heart attack – until he saw the slim black taser in Rogelio's left hand.

The Filipino stood above him, a smirk on his face, before bending over and picking up the Glock 9mm lying on the floor a few inches away. "*Tarantado ka*," Rogelio said, his words dripping with contempt. "You should never have come here."

Rogelio stabbed the taser into his chest. Jimmy screamed as liquid fire flooded his body, and he kept on screaming even as the world dilated into a deep and impenetrable blackness.

***

"What the fuck?"

Jimmy woke up naked on the gurney, his arms and legs strapped down to the bed with leather restraints. A flower of pain bloomed inside his skull and threatened to split it open. The lights shining above him amplified his stabbing headache. His eyesight, blurry at first, came back into focus, like the lens of a faulty camera, and the black phantoms that congregated in the periphery of his vision became solid forms: the surgeons, their mouths concealed behind surgical masks, looked down at him as if he were a piece of meat about to quartered and filleted.

Among them, Rogelio stood, arms crossed, with a smug grin on his face.

"How are you feeling, boss?"

"What's going on?"

"Nothing much," Rogelio replied. "These gentlemen are going to cut you open. They'll take out your kidneys, your lungs, your heart, your liver – anything that will fetch us a good price on the market. Unfortunately, we're a small operation, so we can't afford anaesthetics."

"You little maggot. You lied to me!"

"I do whatever the customer wants. The thing is, you're not my customer."

As soon as Rogelio turned to walk away, Jimmy called out to him in desperation: "Wait," he shouted. "You don't have to do this. We can make a deal. How much do you people want?"

"How much do you think your kidney costs?"

"I – I don't know."

"Ten thousand dollars," Rogelio said. "That's just for your left kidney alone. We have a Korean businessman who's willing to buy both of them. Can you top his price?"

"Yes," Jimmy screamed. "Yes, I can!"

"What about your heart?"

"What?"

"Can you buy it back for twenty thousand?"

"I don't have that kind of money!"

"Your lungs, ten thousand each," Rogelio began ticking off the prices of Jimmy's organs on his fingers. "Your liver, eight thousand. Your bone marrow, fifty thousand. Your eyes, fifteen thousand for both. That's only a rough estimate."

"You can't do this," Jimmy cried out.

"Your brain? Well, that's the only thing we can't use. I can feed it to my dogs, or I can sell it to you for a low price. Give me ten pesos, and you can keep it. How about that?"

"I'm begging you," Jimmy sobbed, "let me go. I won't tell anyone what happened."

"You must think all Filipinos are a bunch of idiots, huh? That you can buy all of us with your American dollars? I can make my own money. I don't need your dollars."

"Please, Rogelio," Jimmy whimpered. "You have a family too, don't you?"

"Think about it this way," Rogelio replied, "once you're gone from their lives, they'll be much safer. Nobody's gonna harm them anymore. You should thank me. I'm doing you a favour."

Jimmy struggled against his restraints, in vain, as Rogelio walked toward the door. "Rogelio!" he screamed, crying. At first, Jimmy felt an overwhelming sense of relief when the driver stopped and looked back at him, until he saw the expression on Rogelio's face: he had the gaze of a man who seemed to have done this sort of thing again and again, without any guilt or remorse.

Only one thing crossed Jimmy's mind then:

Aswang.

Ghouls pretending to be men.

"That ain't even my name."

KAIJU

I should buy her some flowers, Toshiro thought as he inserted one leg into the latex *kaiju* costume. He had never meant to hit Reika, not really, but after noticing another dried speck of egg yolk on one of the dishes, Toshiro backhanded her with enough force to make her nose bleed.

Toshiro kept on reminding her to pre-wash the plates before loading them into the dishwasher. This way, they wouldn't have to waste money by scrubbing and rinsing them again. Couldn't she understand how hard it was to earn a living in today's economy?

If she hadn't been three weeks pregnant, it would've been a lot worse than a slap.

Why did he have to get so angry before anyone took him seriously?

Sighing, Toshiro continued putting on his costume, slipping into the rubber skin of the reptilian creature with ease. As a veteran Tokusatsu actor, he had gotten used to wearing all manner of outfits ranging from the spandex uniforms of intergalactic heroes to radioactive abominations created by monstrous alien races. Most amateur performers needed assistance from other crew members to get ready for a full day of filming at the studio, but not him.

Toshiro preferred to work alone.

Once he'd finished wearing the latex mask of the atomic, fire-breathing, mutant spinosaurus that Hitachi Productions created for "Shin Solarman: Monster Buster," Toshiro took a deep breath and inhaled the musky scent of rubber, allowing it to fill his nostrils. He loved the smell of unwashed latex, even though most people found it quite disgusting.

The synthetic rubber odour, combined with the week-old aroma of dried sweat, created an organic stench that made it seem as if he were stepping into the skin of a living creature. That smell, so unique and pervasive, made it easier for Toshiro to enter the mindset of the *kaiju*.

After completing his daily ritual, Toshiro felt his tense muscles relax.

He couldn't understand why, but every time he slipped into the skin of a giant monster, all his worries, anxiety, and stress melted away. Toshiro never felt any discomfort while playing a *kaiju*, even though the typical costume weighed at least 170 pounds.

At 40 years old, Toshiro had the build of a professional mixed martial artist and was able to bench press more than 250 pounds with ease. Strength training was necessary to move with ease under layers of meticulously sculpted rubber, acrylic paint, and plaster. Without it, he wouldn't have been able to lift even a single finger while wearing the costume. Sadly, nobody ever appreciated the effort Toshiro dedicated to his craft. Even his fellow actors at the studio were baffled by his commitment to playing the role of a villain in a Saturday morning kid's show.

They never understood why he went through such great lengths for this role; what kind of an idiot would dedicate his entire acting career performing as an overgrown lizard? Toshiro couldn't explain that he only felt at ease whenever he wore the skin of a monster and rampaged across a detailed set of miniature houses. As a man, he was nothing more than a two-bit actor, a failure who only entered showbusiness after failing his college entrance exams.

But as a giant, radioactive monster? He was strong. Powerful. Immortal.

It didn't matter that he was only pretending.

***

As usual, Toshiro arrived at the studio an hour earlier than the staff and the production crew to get himself primed and ready for the morning's shoot. He had been reading books written by Lee Strasberg on the Stanislavski Method, and he wondered if he could apply these acting techniques to his performance as a colossal, city-levelling monstrosity.

A short warm-up while clad in the latex costume gave Toshiro the insight he needed to delve into the complex psychology of this grotesque behemoth. Although the show's screenwriters never gave the *kaiju* an actual name, Toshiro insisted on calling it "Barbarilios," a suggestion that the director and his fellow actors laughed at. Still, whenever Toshiro carried out his affective memory exercises, he continued referring to the *kaiju* as Barbarilios, a savage name that implied strength, ferocity, and unyielding rage. Toshiro didn't care that everyone else considered it a joke.

Only a couple of overhead floodlights provided faint sources of illumination across the miniature city built from plywood, styrofoam, and plastic. A scaled-down replica of downtown Tokyo, this diorama contained replicas of the Nakagin Capsule Tower, the Tokyo Skytree and even the hole-in-the-wall ramen shops that populated the city's bustling sidewalks.

Soon, Toshiro thought, all of this would be nothing but ashes and rubble.

As he shuffled across the main street toward a scaled-down Tokyo Tower, Toshiro imagined the destruction he would cause when the cameras started rolling. Engineered pyrotechnics would erupt all around him, creating a cacophony of jarring sounds, noises, and lights.

Toshiro could still remember the first time he had ever stepped foot in this studio—the mayhem that erupted when he brawled with the actor who played the role of Shin Solarman. The fight scene had been choreographed, of course, but that didn't diminish the intensity of the experience, especially when they tossed each other into the miniature buildings, sending chunks of plywood, plaster, and styrofoam flying in every direction.

During those moments, Toshiro felt more alive than alive, more human than human – a bizarre warmth engulfed his entire body, flooding his veins with an unusual jolt of adrenaline. That familiar, all-consuming fury was something that Toshiro lived with every day. Yes, this anger, this rage, brought him closer to Barbarilios. Like the *kaiju* itself, he also hated human beings.

He hated them for their adherence to suffocating social norms that forced failed salarymen and shut-ins to commit suicide; hated them for their dull, uninspiring lives spent being shuttled in packed trains like cattle to their workplaces; hated them for not noticing his talent.

How many times had he looked upon the National Diet building and prayed for the power to tear it all down and pound its walls into powdered concrete and glass? How many times had he wished he could grab the Tokyo Tower, uproot it like a weed, and break it in half upon his knee? As a human being, Toshiro could never hope to accomplish this sort of wanton destruction. But as a monster, as Barbarilios, he could channel his pent-up rage into a creative outlet.

With slow, lurching steps, Toshiro walked across the facsimile of the Tokyo metropolis, revelling in his height and power. How easy it would be to crush these buildings, to trample them beneath the heel of Barbarilios, to scatter these fragile structures built by human hands and show this naive and frivolous species the meaninglessness of their existence against the might of nature.

The sharp clack of overhead shutters brought Toshiro out of his reverie; glancing about, he had to shield his eyes from the outflow of brightness that spilled forth from the floodlights. Goddammit, Toshiro thought, the crew wasn't supposed to be there yet! He had barely gotten warmed up, and already some idiot of a technician was disturbing his affective memory exercise.

How was he supposed to work under these conditions?

"Who's there?" Toshiro shouted.

Nobody replied.

After his eyes had gotten used to the light, he removed the forearm shielding his face and glanced around, searching for the smartass who was probably playing a prank on him. Instead of seeing the familiar, industrial layout of the studio – with its pipes and wires and ventilation – Toshiro found himself staring at a bright midday sky and the silhouette of Mount Fuji.

What the hell was going on?

Stunned, Toshiro could do nothing but look at his surroundings.

Well, goddamn, he thought, I didn't know we had the budget to generate this level of special effects. Before he could continue admiring the obviously holographic backdrop of the *Tokusatsu* set, Toshiro heard an almost inaudible scream coming from behind him.

The voice, which sounded female, was so tiny and so faint that he wouldn't have been able to find its source if the unseen woman hadn't screamed again. When Toshiro looked down at his feet, he then saw, to his surprise and confusion, an absurdly small person, no more than five centimetres in height, standing on the street of the Tokyo diorama.

The minuscule woman had dropped her bag of groceries and kept on screaming and screaming as she stared up at Toshiro's massive bulk. Still bewildered by the sight of a miniature housewife screeching in sheer terror, Toshiro crouched so that could get a better glance.

The woman looked so real, so natural, he almost thought that she was an actual person.

He wondered how much money the company had spent to craft such a convincing miniature animatronic puppet. He wasn't even sure it was possible to produce something so life-like; in his ten years of working as a *Tokusatsu* actor, Toshiro had never seen anything quite so realistic.

How did the special effects crew create a marionette like this?

Another scream, this time coming from a few metres away, made Toshiro turn his head; there, on the ground, stood another puppet, a male one. Like its female counterpart, the miniature man pointed up and shouted, "*Kaiju! Kaiju!*" with sheer, unbridled terror.

The sight of it made Toshiro laugh out loud.

His cackling reverberated across the avenue, shaking loose dust from the nearby buildings.

While enjoying the sight of these shrieking puppets, Toshiro noticed that more and more animatronic humans emerged, each one handcrafted with meticulous detail and attention to character. No two replicas looked alike. Some were middle-aged office workers; others were high school students on their way to school. There were also a few labourers wearing hard hats standing alongside kindergarten students accompanied by their shocked and dumbstruck mothers.

Some fled from Toshiro while others stood frozen, rigid like animals standing before an oncoming truck's headlights, unable to move, unable to do anything but tremble in fear. A coil of anxiety unfurled itself inside Toshiro's stomach. These things had to be puppets, right?

And yet, their reactions, their terror at seeing him, seemed so utterly convincing, so wholly human, that he couldn't help but doubt his own convictions.

There was only one way to find out if these things were real or not – and so Toshiro reached down with his clawed hand and tried to pluck one of the animatronic puppets from the ground.

This, however, was easier said than done.

The little things scurried about and evaded his grasp.

Moving around in the *kaiju* costume prevented Toshiro from doing more delicate tasks. Most of the crowd that gathered on the street managed to run away, shrieking in fright, warning every other person they met to flee from the gargantuan actor in a latex costume. Frustrated, Toshiro rose, then lumbered onward, accidentally smashing through a nearby building.

The set designer would most likely kick his ass once they saw the kind of destruction that he had caused while "warming up." *Screw them*, Toshiro thought. He didn't give a shit anymore.

Toshiro chased the fleeing pedestrians, most of whom scattered into different directions. Eventually, one of the miniature humans tripped, and Toshiro managed to snag him up. The puppet, who was a middle-aged balding man dressed in a business suit, cried out for someone to help him.

Holy shit, these things look so real! Toshiro thought.

He considered bringing one back home and perhaps keep it inside an aquarium, something to brag about when his drinking buddies visited in the future. The balding businessman, tears streaming down his eyes, squirmed and struggled to escape. The animatronic puppet looked almost as if he were turning mad with fear as he pleaded with Toshiro to spare his life.

At first, after seeing the simulated fear in the animatronic puppet's eyes, Toshiro considered just dropping him back on the ground and letting him go. He had to remind himself that this doll, this toy, wasn't human, and he was going to prove that by taking it apart.

Toshiro pinched the small businessman's left arm and pulled. The puppet gave loud, unrelenting wails of agony; nevertheless, Toshiro continued trying to pop out the man's arm. He couldn't understand why it was giving so much resistance. Usually, puppets such as these could be easily dismantled and pulled apart for easy cleaning and maintenance.

Grunting, Toshiro gave a bit more effort, and soon enough, the limb began to give way.

A crunching sound, like that of a knife cutting through a head of cabbage, was quickly followed by a sickening noise which sounded like wet seaweed being pulled apart. Eventually, Toshiro managed to tear the arm off, but instead of seeing a plastic ball joint protruding from the severed limb, he noticed a geyser of bright, red ink gushing out of the shoulder.

The puppet, seemingly in pain, convulsed, as if going into shock.

For a moment, Toshiro hesitated.

What kind of puppet bleeds red ink?

No, he said to himself, this has got to be one of those ultra-realistic models—the kind that bled whenever they get squished or stepped on. It seemed a little bit too extreme to develop them for a kid's show, but then again, the rise of violence in most *Tokusatsu* series wasn't unusual.

Even the proliferation of lewd anime with hyper-violent imagery had become accepted by Japanese society. Nobody ever blinked an eye whenever a character was killed in a gruesome manner on screen. It saddened Toshiro that Shin Solarman would soon follow the direction of these ultra-violent shows, but what else could he do? The thought of the world of *Tokusatsu* leaving him behind angered Toshiro even more, and he decided to take out that anger on the puppet that kept on giving a grotesque death spasm in his closed fist. Time to stop this nonsense, he thought.

Now let's see how you were made.

Gripping the animatronic businessman's head between his clawed thumb and forefinger, Toshiro gave a slight squeeze before turning it as if he were unscrewing the cap of a Calpis bottle.

By this time, the puppet had stopped squirming, and Toshiro kept on twisting the miniature person's head until, inevitably, he managed to pull it off. A geyser of fake blood gushed out of the man's throat, painting some of the buildings crimson. Still, Toshiro couldn't find any plastic parts, no wires or complicated circuit boards to explain how the puppet moved. Frustrated, he tore into the animatronic human in his desperate search for a battery pack, a motor, something that could prove to him that this thing was nothing more than a facsimile of a person.

With furious zeal, Toshiro started tearing off his other limbs, ripping them from their sockets one by one, until the puppet had been reduced to a blood-soaked lump in his hands.

And when nothing of the man's arms and legs remained, he ripped the torso apart, piece by piece. He still couldn't see any batteries, couldn't see any wires. Only the puppet's innards, its intestines, lungs, and its heart plopped out and dropped to the asphalt below.

He couldn't believe his eyes.

"Hey!" Toshiro shouted. "This isn't funny anymore!"

Annoyed, but still shaken, Toshiro gripped the back of his neck and tried to tear off the Barbarilios headgear. He didn't care about getting paid, he just wanted to leave the studio. This nonsense had gone on for far too long. However, for some strange reason, the mask wouldn't budge at all.

It remained glued to his head, unwilling to be removed. Toshiro tried to pull on it even harder, grunting like a beast as he did so. Still, the mask wouldn't give. He then looked for the costume's seam that lay somewhere between his neck and the *kaiju*'s shoulder blades. To his horror, he just couldn't find it.

The seam had to be there. Maybe the heat of the overhead lights had fused the latex mask to the costume. If he couldn't find the region where the headpiece joined the body, then he would tear open a new one. Upon digging his claws into the costume's rubbery flesh, Toshiro felt agony crawl down the length of his chest. The pain, however, fuelled his anger.

He pulled and pulled at the skin until the searing ache became too much, and he had no choice but to give up. Panting, Toshiro looked at his hands. They were now covered with a sickly green ichor that gave off an offensive smell, like sewage from a clogged toilet.

Then, he stared at his chest and saw the holes he had punctured in the costume.

The same greenish fluid flowed out of the lacerations, oozing like blood, and Toshiro couldn't stave off the hysteria that had threatened to overwhelm him minutes ago. This was happening – this was really happening. He chuckled, insanely, at the thought.

Somehow, he had become Barbarilios.

Toshiro didn't have time to contemplate his situation. The deafening blare of police and ambulance sirens disturbed him, and he then noticed a cadre of patrol cruisers swarming into the avenue and surrounding him on all sides. They formed a barrier around him with their vehicles; the officers stepped out of the cars, then pointed their tiny pistols and shotguns at him.

Even from such a height, Toshiro could sense the fear of the police officers, and could see their frightened eyes as they stared at him. This was the first time they had ever seen a *kaiju* in the flesh. Unlike the Tokusatsu shows that Toshiro acted in, there was no giant superhero coming to the rescue, no Shin Solarman fighting on humanity's behalf. Some of the officers looked away from the kaiju and saw the pieces of the businessman that Toshiro had ripped apart.

An awful silence descended upon the street as they all stared at the chunks of meat and flesh scattered across the asphalt. The sight spurred animalistic violence within them, and before Toshiro could react, a hail of gunfire started hitting him. It wasn't enough to wound him – not gravely anyway – but it felt as if he were being bitten by a swarm of killer wasps armed with toxic stingers.

Instinctively, Toshiro kicked some of the patrol cars standing in his way, sending chunks of metal and screaming human beings flying in every direction. A few officers got splattered against the walls of the condominiums and apartment complexes nearby from the sheer force of Toshiro's blow, leaving irregular patterns of blood that looked, strangely, like Rorschach blots.

Oh God, Toshiro thought, I just killed them.

I killed other people.

***

Toshiro ran.

Earth-shaking footfalls sent buses jack-knifing in the air as Toshiro fled. Chunks of concrete debris scattered haphazardly in various directions. Some of the rubble smashed into nearby buildings, creating massive holes. An overpass blocking Toshiro's path crumbled like shortbread.

Vehicles fell onto the street below, squashing the hapless pedestrians underneath.

Glancing backward, Toshiro noticed the surviving police officers chasing him through the bedlam on their patrol cruisers; the sound of gunfire and sirens followed as he fled. This had to be a dream, Toshiro thought, a waking nightmare. None of what was happening had to be real.

Before he could take another step, however, a crippling jolt of electricity rippled up his spine; roaring, Toshiro lost his balance and fell sideways. The impact of his collapse sent shockwaves billowing outward with enough force to topple telephone poles in the vicinity.

What's happening to me? Toshiro thought.

As he rolled on the ground, wailing, he felt thousands upon thousands of small, vicious knives stabbing into the outer layer of his epidermis. He felt his bones reshaping themselves into twisted, inhuman angles, heard ligaments and muscles snapping like high tension wires.

His veins felt like they were being filled with battery acid, corrosive and deadly, melting any semblance of his former humanity and injecting him with another, more insidious essence—something darker, hungrier, an elder thing born from some unknown and sinister abyss.

In that instant, as his body underwent a grotesque and abominable change, an awful thought went through Toshiro's mind like the tip of a heated knife slowly piercing raw meat:

What if this *wasn't* a nightmare? What if he was actually a *kaiju* who dreamt that he was human? And what if that dream was now over, and the *kaiju* was finally awake?

When the pain gradually subsided, Toshiro tried to rise, but instead of walking on two feet, as usual, he could only slouch forward, like a hunchback, his crooked arms now bent at his sides, unable to stretch themselves out. Toshiro tried to keep himself standing; however, the bulk of his weight, and the way his newfound body was made, couldn't keep him upright for very long.

He fell forward, crushing a busload of people like pomegranates inside a crate.

Struggling once more to rise, Toshiro found that he could no longer stand straight.

An overwhelming sense of terror washed over him like a black tide when he realised that he could feel sensations coming from the *kaiju* costume's latex tail. Almost by instinct, Toshiro discovered that he could move the appendage from side-to-side. Despite this horrible realisation, Toshiro knew that he couldn't afford to stay still, especially with the sound of police sirens and the whirring of unseen assault helicopters coming closer and closer to his position.

Using the tail as a counterweight, Toshiro managed to keep himself balanced. Lurching, he started moving unnaturally, his body undulating in an almost snake-like motion while his two hind legs propelled him. As he went, Toshiro barrelled through houses, buildings, bridges, crushing structures underfoot. He had only one thing in his mind:

To see his wife. Toshiro just wanted to see his Reika again.

Surely, she would still recognize him despite his monstrous appearance. Reika wouldn't run away from him in fear like the others. She had always been by his side, no matter how cruel or hurtful he'd been. Toshiro felt a twinge of guilt as he remembered how he'd hurt Reika.

He wanted to say sorry.

He wanted to buy her roses.

Reika, sweetheart, Toshiro thought. I'm coming home.

***

The street remained as Toshiro remembered—quaint and unassuming, a suburb that anyone can see in any city in Japan. This time, instead of being greeted by birdsong and the sounds of children playing at the neighbourhood park, the familiar sounds of this place he once called home were replaced by the ear-piercing wails of air-raid beacons piercing the midday air. The street was devoid of all life, with most of the populace probably hiding in nearby underground shelters.

Although Toshiro had outrun the combined forces of the military and the police that were coming after him, he still knew that there wasn't much time before they'd arrive.

Of course, he also knew that such puny firearms wouldn't hurt him, but he was more worried about the chaos that would ensue. As much as possible, Toshiro didn't want Reika to get caught in the crossfire since he wasn't sure he'd be able to control himself.

Toshiro didn't bother reading the tiny writings on the street signs, since they were too small for his eyes to comprehend. Instead, he relied on his memory and searched for landmarks and that would lead him back to the two-bedroom apartment that he had been renting. Soon enough, he spotted the 10-story residential building with its unassuming brown stucco facade. He hoped that Reika was there. Toshiro wasn't sure what good it would do if his wife saw him like this. He imagined, insanely, one of those fairy tales where the kiss of a princess would set the frog, or the beast, or the wolf free from its prison of flesh and transform him into a prince. Human again. Whole again.

Crouching low, Toshiro clumsily peeked through the windows of the apartment's third floor and searched for any sign of his wife. Their room, unfortunately, lay empty. Everything inside looked fake, like a dollhouse constructed to accommodate artificial people made from plastic.

Despite his size, Toshiro could still make out some of the objects within the area: tables, chairs, and other furniture were placed in orderly formations across the living room. Toshiro had always been a stickler for cleanliness, and Reika tried her best to accommodate his demands.

It was only then that Toshiro began to appreciate his wife's willingness to please him.

He wondered, for a brief second, if Reika did so out of love, or out of fear.

Reika, Toshiro thought, where are you?

Turning his head slowly, Toshiro noticed a woman standing in the hallway of the third floor, her back pinned against the wall, eyes wide. It was his wife, Reika; sweet, and patient Reika.

She wore her hair in a ponytail, just like always, giving her a beautiful quietude that Toshiro used to love before. Before what, exactly? When did he start hating her so much, and why?

Of course, Reika wouldn't recognize him, not as he appeared, but if she could only remember his voice, if she could only hear him say her name, then everything would be all right.

Toshiro opened his mouth and tried to speak; he tried to whisper Reika's name. Instead of words of love and fidelity spilling forth from his maw, nothing came but the rough, jagged growls of a vicious beast, unintelligible and frightening. Again, he attempted to form words with his jaws, only to fail and release grunts of frustration that made the windows of the apartment tremble. Toshiro's grunts and moans only made Reika scramble closer to the wall.

She closed her eyes tightly and covered both ears with her hands.

Reika! Toshiro tried to shout. Reika! Don't be scared!

I'm not gonna hurt you!

His words, however, only produced monstrous howls and moans that sounded so threatening and grotesque. Toshiro had to stop after recognizing the futility of his endeavour.

Perhaps, he thought, stepping back from the apartment, he deserved this punishment. He was once, after all, a monster in human form who treated his wife with viciousness.

Nothing much had changed except for his size.

Toshiro trudged away from the apartment. If he could have wept, he would've, but he wasn't even sure if that was something a *kaiju* was capable of doing. As he lumbered off toward no particular direction, Toshiro wondered where else he could go. The mountains? The sea?

Would he ever find a place to call home again?

Before he could advance more than a few hundred metres, however, Toshiro saw, in the distant horizon, a fleet of Mitsubishi F2 fighter planes sweeping over the clouds, tearing up the sky in his direction, leaving streaks of tattered condensation in their wake. Thanks to his now enhanced hearing abilities, he could hear the low rumble of their engines as they swarmed closer and closer in perfect formation. There were, at least by Toshiro's estimation, more than fifty or so F2 fighters bearing primed ASM-1 air-to-ground missiles.

Soon, Toshiro knew they would bring hellfire and fury down upon his head.

Meanwhile, at ground level, Toshiro spotted a cloud of dust billowing a few kilometres away. The fog almost obscured and camouflaged a battalion of Type 10 battle tanks armed with surface-to-air rocket launchers. How many were there, exactly? Sixty? A hundred? Toshiro couldn't tell. All he knew for certain was that they were about to launch their giant-killing weapons at him in a matter of minutes and this tranquil neighbourhood would turn into a sea of flames.

And Reika would be caught in the crossfire along with their unborn son.

Toshiro couldn't let that happen.

At that moment, he felt pure, heroic, as if he had been born specifically for this one purpose alone: to protect his wife from those who wanted to harm her and their child. Including himself.

Embracing the rage that had built up within him, Toshiro charged towards the army, bellowing furiously—a beast stirring from its centuries-long slumber, towering above all the fragile works and cities of men.

THE LAST CONFESSION OF DOTTORE GEPPETTO

I killed my own son.

For ten years, I tracked him down from town to town, village to village, city to city. In his wake, he left behind nothing but misery, pain, and death. Children died wherever he went, their hearts ripped from their chests, bodies split open in a grotesque display of senseless violence.

I did not know, at first, what he was after; I only knew that I had to stop him.

In the autumn of 1812, a most terrible year of warfare and disease, I arrived in the backwater village of Ludica. There were rumours that a demon roamed the woods surrounding this hamlet, preying on children who wandered at night. While the world grappled with its calamities, I followed the trail of corpses, armed only with pistol and dagger, with sorrow and regret.

I created this demon.

This creature.

Only *I* could end its madness.

***

When I arrived in the village, I noticed how strangely dark and silent it was.

The torches and lamps of nearby houses remained unlit, their windows closed and the doors barred shut. No wagons traversed the unpaved dirt roads of Ludica. The usual clopping of hooves and the idle chatter of merchants and villagers could no longer be heard anywhere in the now desolate town square.

It was as if no one was living there, as if all of its inhabitants had vanished overnight.

At first, I thought that the village had been abandoned until I saw a group of night-watchmen walking down the main avenue, armed with lanterns and muskets. Upon seeing me, a stranger, the guards raised their guns. I held my hands up and told them that I meant no harm.

86

I was merely an old man, lost and confused, simply trying to make his way to Naples to see his grandchildren. The watchmen, still suspicious, seemed to reluctantly accept this explanation and pointed me to an inn where I could rest and eat. However, they left me with a strict warning to leave upon the break of dawn. Feigning ignorance, I asked them why the town was so empty, so devoid of noise and laughter.

"A demon," one of the guards said in a hushed voice, "a creature from the depths of hell is stalking the countryside". It had already butchered six of their children, along with an elderly wool merchant who had caught a glimpse of the monstrous thing that killed her grandson. Before dying from her horrific injuries, the poor woman revealed to the villagers the appearance of the creature: it was an automaton, a fiend made of steel, somehow given life by some forbidden, infernal alchemy.

They were describing my son.

My dearest boy.

I had to turn away to wipe the tears threatening to spill from my eyes. When one of the guards asked if something was the matter, I answered that the thought of such tragedies happening in this peaceful little town was too much for an old heart like mine to bear. The watchmen thanked me for my grief and my condolences. Afterwards, they then told me to seek shelter at once, lest the demon catch me walking the streets of Ludica alone.

I tipped my hat to them in gratitude.

The patrol then went on its way, leaving me alone in that cold, godforsaken street. Instead of heeding their advice, I made haste and turned towards another road that led to the outskirts of Ludica. During my travels, I had heard rumours of a ruined chapel located in the forest, a place that the townsfolk considered unhallowed ground where fiends gathered.

It was the perfect place for a demon to hide.

With only the light of a gibbous moon guiding my way, I followed the weed-choked path that led deeper and deeper into the benighted regions of the forest. Nothing frightened me. Not anymore. Sorrow had stripped terror from my heart and left nothing but despair in its place. The thought of bandits hiding in the undergrowth inspired only indifference. I had nothing left to give except my life, such as it is, and even that was worth almost nothing. Demons, too, did not stoke any of my innermost fears, for had I not created a demon with these calloused, arthritic hands?

***

I walked, alone, a frail old man in the haunted, shadow-shrouded forest, wishing only to die. But such a mercy would not be granted to a blasphemer like myself by the powers of Heaven, for I still had a penance to perform. It had not always been like this. Before I became a vagrant, I was an engineer, a celebrated toymaker for the noble families of old and marvellous Venice.

As a craftsman and an artist of the highest calibre, I was well-known for creating trinkets and mechanical animals that were so life-like, so meticulously designed, they were often mistaken for sentient beings by my royal patrons. None of them knew of my insidious connection to the surgical genius, the Baron Victor Frankenstein, who died in the cold regions of the North Pole while hunting down a monstrosity he had cobbled together from various corpses.

While we were still young students in the University of Ingolstadt, the Baron and I often mused upon the meaning of life, death, and the power of science and medicine to manipulate natural processes. Driven by the death of his mother, Baron Frankenstein wanted to see if he could, in some way, give life to non-living matter. His experiments intrigued me and so I assisted my friend in his abhorrent and sacrilegious task of reanimating long-dead human beings.

But while he wanted to defeat death, I wanted to do so much more—Victor couldn't see the potential in the grand work we had undertaken. He wanted to cure death. He wanted to save humanity from the shadow of the abyss. I wanted to create a new species altogether – a creature that would soon replace the flawed and violent race of mankind.

Ultimately, it was this difference of opinion that soon drove us apart.

Baron Frankenstein went his separate way and I continued my research independently. While creating useless but miraculous toys for the mewling brats of counts and countesses, I managed to amass a sizable fortune, one that allowed me to buy the materials needed to create my masterwork. During this period of trial and error, I learned from various sources about the death of my dear friend and colleague, and I vowed that I would continue the work we had started.

But unlike the ingenious Baron Frankenstein, who used corpses to create a ravening golem, I wanted to construct my precious son from metal. Human flesh is such a crude material, full of diseases and imperfections. Was it any wonder, then, that my friend's creation turned out to be a ghastly fiend capable of only murder? He gave it a human mind. He gave it a human heart.

My son would be different from his.

This child, I thought, would be pure.

He would be freed from the constraints of the human form. My son would know no disease, no pain, no death. His indestructible body would be operated by an electric dynamo for a heart and a mechanical brain that could think, and reason, and calculate more efficiently than a human being's mind—a consciousness unfettered by the foolishness of mankind.

My son would know no hatred.

No love.

It would only know truth, logic, and reason.

I thought that I had created an angel.

How utterly foolish I was.

***

After what seemed like hours upon hours of walking aimlessly through the forest, I chanced upon the grove where the forbidden chapel was situated. On the ground, placed in a grotesque circle, lay the naked, decomposing, and headless bodies of several children. They seem to have been dead for almost a week or so, in my rough estimation, and a foul, rotten stench rose up from the mutilated cadavers. Fighting the instinct to vomit, I knelt down and examined the corpses while covering my nose and mouth with the hem of a patched and tattered cloak hanging from my thin shoulders.

Each of the dead boys had been flayed, expertly skinned, leaving nothing behind save for the greenish-brown cords of rotting and fly-ridden muscle fibres.

I could only hope that they had died before the foul deed was performed upon their helpless bodies. Like the countless victims I had encountered during my decade-long search, they had their internal organs removed, their heart, lungs, kidneys, and livers extracted with surgical precision.

The reasons behind this, I didn't know, and I didn't want to know, for only an inhuman and diabolical mind would perpetrate such a despicable act of sheer lunacy. And yet, I had to ask myself:

was it truly madness that guided the hand of my once beloved son?

Surely, there had to be a perfectly reasonable explanation for such cruelty.

And why not?

Rationality is a monstrous device capable of explaining away murderous deeds.

Logic and reason had often been used to justify atrocities perpetrated throughout the history of our doomed race. Was Napoleon not reasonable, and logical, and sane, when he declared war upon the Empire of Russia? Reasonable men, civilised men, had destroyed the grand palaces and temples of the Aztecs. It was reason that drove the armies of our Great Emperor Napoleon to march across Europe, killing, stealing, and raping in a ceaseless orgy of wanton destruction.

On trembling legs, I rose from the ground, before pulling out the flintlock pistol from my coat. The cold weight of the handgun felt comforting, familiar, in my hand. It reminded me of a hammer. It reminded me of the good days, the productive days, when all I needed was solitude and a space to work my craft. I am no soldier. I am a tinkerer. A fixer.

In the past, I once told Baron Frankenstein that the world's problems could only be solved by human intellect, not by bullets and gunpowder. Those days are long gone.

I wrapped the coat tightly around my body to stave off the biting midnight chill.

Though I tried to steady myself, I could not stop the shaking of my aching, unsteady bones. Time seemed to slow down at an unbearable pace as I took a few tentative steps toward the threshold of the crumbling chapel. This place of worship, now a nest of ill rumours and evil spirits, looked old, older than I could reckon even with my prodigious knowledge of architectural styles of the past few centuries. That it was Christian, I had no doubt, for a crumbling limestone cross sat atop its vine-choked rooftop. Whatever holiness that this artefact once possessed, I prayed that it would protect me from the fiendish presence that lurked within the desolate chapel.

As a man of science, I trusted only in the things that my senses could see, smell, hear, and touch. I thought that primordial evil was nothing but mere superstition, a fairy tale concocted by lesser minds to comprehend the strangeness of the physical world around them.

But now, I have seen the error of my judgement. Evil exists. I had seen it. I had felt it.

I had followed it for ten years. I had a duty to stop it.

Once and for all.

***

The pockmarked wooden gate leading into the darkened interior of the chapel was slightly ajar, as if whoever or whatever waited inside had been expecting me to arrive. Gripping the pistol, I slipped through the gap between the doors, which was big enough to allow a frail, elderly man to slip through. Upon crossing the threshold, I discovered that the interior of the main hallway was illuminated by torches along with half-melted and dying wax candles.

How I wished that God had blinded me in that instant, for I saw, in that accursed place, a gallery of horrors that made my consciousness buckle and almost break. On each pillar flanking the cobwebbed pews, the flayed corpses of male and female children – each one no more than ten years old – had been crucified and displayed like grotesque statues in a museum of the damned.

Unlike the carcasses left outside, however, these ones possessed all their organs and innards. A shattering thought came to me: these victims weren't killed to satisfy sadistic impulses. They were being studied, surgically deconstructed, as if they were anatomical specimens.

My son, for some unfathomable purpose, had killed these children for purely academic and scientific pursuits. Walking down the aisle, I threw sharp glances at the nearby pews and saw, to my disgust, dusty glass jars that contained organs swimming in a greenish semi-transparent soup:

hearts, livers, kidneys, lungs, intestines, all of them preserved for examination and study.

Then, from a corner of the hall, someone whispered:

"Father?"

I recognized that voice; the lithe, lilting tone that gave me such joy in the past only sent a chill dread crawling across my spine like a monstrous centipede. Had it truly been a decade since he had escaped my workshop to spread havoc across this war-ravaged continent? Hearing him again, I wondered if it were possible, somehow, to save him, to recreate his functions and recalibrate his mind so that corruption would never tarnish his mechanical consciousness again.

"My boy," I said softly. "What have you done?"

"Only what you have failed to achieve," my son replied, his voice echoing against the walls. "I have become like you, Dottore Geppetto: a human being in thought and design."

"You were perfect!" I shouted, weeping, my voice cracking. "You were everything that I have ever dreamt of being! I created you to replace us! To be better than us!"

"Oh, Father," he replied from the shadows. "You do not see the glorious nature of the human species. But I have. You are like stars dancing in the infinite blackness of this lonesome cosmos: bright, effervescent, fleeting. The god who created you must have loved you deeply."

From behind, I could hear footsteps, coupled with the sound of blood hitting the stone floor.

"I have studied the human form, and with each specimen that I had disassembled, I grew only more confused. Although they retained the same number of organs, and nerves, and vital functions, their shapes, colours, and details varied from one person to the next."

I drew in a ragged breath and closed my eyes.

There was such innocence in his words.

Such curiosity.

Of course. I had designed him to be without love, or hatred, or fear.

He was an angel, and how could, lowly, confused, frightened creatures such as us comprehend the thoughts of the sinless? He was truly perfect. This was perfection at work.

"Then, I realised that I did not possess the thing that you humans so thoughtlessly take for granted: your souls. No matter how many children I tore apart, I couldn't find any traces of this wondrous, wondrous thing, this vital essence, that sets you apart from a machine like me."

"There is no such thing as a soul."

"That is where you are mistaken," he said, chuckling. Oh, merciful God, I had never heard him laugh before. "Look upon me, Father, and I will show you what the soul looks like."

Slowly, so slowly, I turned.

And then I saw him.

He was no longer a machine.

Far from it.

"Aren't you proud of me, Papa?"

In the dimly-lit room, I saw, to my horror and great despair, that he had undergone an ingenious self-surgery which grafted the skins, the muscles, and the organs of his victims to his mechanical body. Blood dripped from the suture wounds on the surface of his makeshift skin.

It was a mockery.

A grotesque parody of the human body.

In the centre of his chest, encased within a glass jar, was a beating heart floating in a translucent and ochre-coloured substance. Spreading his fleshy arms wide, as if asking for an embrace, my son staggered toward me, grinned madly, and then said:

"I've become a real boy."

JURAMENTADO

On November 14, 1907, a platoon of soldiers led by Lieutenant John Brooder entered Cotabato's hinterlands. They never returned. 38 years later, during the Second World War, his journal was discovered after the liberation of Mindanao from the Japanese Imperial Forces.

***

My Dearest Lisa,

This will be my final letter.

Our situation in Mindanao is dire, and I see no hope of coming home alive. We have been defeated. That, I cannot deny. But it was not for lack of skill or courage that my men were slain, and our forces scattered, overcome by an enemy that cannot be touched by steel or gunpowder.

I do not have much time. As best as possible, I will try to recount the circumstances that brought us to this juncture. On August 30, 1907, we received calls for aid from the soldiers stationed at our garrison along the benighted forests of Cotabato. They were under constant, nightly attack and had lost almost half of their troop strength. In a message addressed to Major General Leonard Wood, Lieutenant David Billings of the 6th Infantry Regiment wrote about nighttime chanting coming from the woods, accompanied by the wild beating of drums and other, less fathomable noises. These rituals, reminiscent of the Ghost Dances performed by the Lakota tribesmen, preceded vicious midnight assaults that whittled down the garrison's defences.

The Major General ordered us to relieve Lieutenant Billings, who seemed on the verge of lunacy after half-a-year of guarding the Tampakan encampment. We were tasked to hold the position and quell any signs of rebellion among the populace. The platoon of soldiers under my command, totaling 45 in strength, was composed of veterans from the Battle of Wounded Knee. Two capable commanders assisted me in this mission: Sergeant Caleb Mossworth and Sergeant Thomas Gillman. Each of us led three squads of 15 men personally handpicked from a choice selection of specialists. Regardless of their backgrounds, my soldiers all had one thing in common:

They knew how to hunt Indians.

During our march to Tampakan, the annual monsoon made the unpaved dirt roads arduous to cross. We trudged through pathways caked with mud that had the consistency of quicksand. Our platoon would not have been able to navigate these treacherous trails teeming with snakes, leeches, and other hidden dangers if our companion, a Christian native named Pablo, did not guide us.

Upon arriving, we found the garrison in a severe state of disrepair. The soldiers looked as if they hadn't slept in weeks, their eyes glazed and anxious. Lieutenant Billings himself had the hollow stare of a man suffering from shell shock. Although he expressed relief at seeing fellow Americans, Billings was also more than eager to leave that accursed place.

In our debriefing, the Lieutenant described tales of lunatic singing that rose above the trees at night. Afterward, the natives would swarm out from the forest, armed with spears, bows, and arrows. Billings and his men managed to repel the savages time and again, but when morning came, they found no corpses, no signs of attack. The nightly raids continued for six months, causing mounting losses. Billings claimed that he saw silhouettes of giant, nameless things skulking in the forest, their eyes glowing red as rubies in the midnight gloom. At the time, I blamed these feverish testimonies on fatigue, hallucinations caused by restless nights, hunger, and disease.

After Billings and his remaining men left for the relative safety and comfort of Manila, we spent weeks waiting for word from the Major General. During this time, my thoughts were filled with memories of you, my dear Lisa. In moments of idleness, I would close my eyes and recall the first time we met in your father's ballroom, how you danced so gracefully with a jonquil tucked in your hair. Such fleeting visions kept me from losing my nerve, especially in the darkness that came after sunset.

That was when the chanting started.

First came the drumbeats, a faint, percussive thumping that grew with intensity, soon joined by the shrill notes of reed pipes playing a discordant and utterly alien melody. To call this cacophony "music" would be blasphemous, for it held nothing in common with intricate compositions of Bach or Mozart. Blessedly, however, no attacks transpired during or after this unsettling ritual. It seemed that the savages befouling the woodland with their grotesque ceremonies and heathen witchcraft only served to fluster our spirits and weaken our resolve.

***

"We have to act," Caleb Mossworth said as we sat around an open fire in the garrison's courtyard at midnight. Thomas Gillman nodded his assent while our guide, Pablo, remained unspeaking. A pot of boiling Batangueno coffee somewhat lifted our downcast spirits, but the incessant howls and shrieks of joy coming from the forest kept our dispositions morose.

"What do you suggest?" I asked.

"It's only a matter of time before they attack. We can hold out for two or three days. But after that," Thomas trailed off. I knew exactly what he implied. With our dwindling supplies, we would have to eventually hunt and forage for food in the woodland.

"So we strike now, take the initiative," Caleb replied.

"You know these lands better than us, Pablo," I said. "What say you?"

"I think we should call for reinforcements, Señor Brooder," Pablo replied.

"Why?"

"The tribesmen in those hills aren't like the ones in Bud Dajo. Blades cannot cut them. Bullets will not stop them. They charge into battle wielding curved swords, wearing nothing but curses tattooed on their skins. The Peninsulares called them the Juramentado. Oath-Keepers."

"You believe this horseshit, John?" Caleb asked, scoffing.

Pablo's eyes flared, but he held his tongue.

"Tell me more about them, these Oath-Keepers," I told Pablo, amused.

"The Juramentado have lived in these woods before Datu Sikatuna swore a blood oath with Miguel Lopez de Legaspi. They are an old, old people, their lineage stretching back to the witch cults of ancient and fabled Srivijaya. Legend has it that they pledged allegiance to a terrible god that dwells beneath Mount Matutum, selling their souls in exchange for immortality."

"What sort of god?" I asked. "Are they not Muslim?"

"Oh, no. Not at all," Pablo replied. "The Juramentado pray to a giant woman whose face is so horrifying, to look upon it would mean certain death. I cannot speak her name. She lives in a dark house under the earth with her thousands of children, whom she nurses with poisonous milk dripping from her leprous breasts. There, in the corpse-city of Gimokodan, they wait and breed until the time comes when the stars are right. Only then will they rise and reclaim what's theirs."

"Reclaim what, exactly?" Thomas asked.

"Why, this land, of course. And everything on it."

Caleb and Thomas began to laugh. Pablo, however, did not protest. He didn't even seem embarrassed by the mockery he received from my adjutants. Pablo merely stared at them.

"Pablo, this nation and its citizens are now under the United States of America's protection," I said calmly, without spite or ridicule. "I cannot allow such pagan barbarism to fester unchecked, or else it will inspire rebellion in the hearts of our little brown brothers."

Pablo looked away from us and toward the forest's direction, where the maddening cries and rapturous shrieks of the Juramentado continued unabated. "Very well, Señor Brooder," he replied. "But we had best move at daybreak. The forest can be murderous come nightfall."

At dawn, we set off southward in the direction of Mount Matutum. The sky had an ashen pallor, while pregnant clouds hung heavy above us, threatening to unleash a downpour of biting rain. As a precaution, we left 10 soldiers to guard the garrison, with instructions to report back to the Major General if our mission went awry. 20 riflemen and five cavalry riders marched with us, along with two carriages bearing armaments, ammunition, and other provisions. I did not expect us to spend more than three days afield, but we carried enough supplies to last a week.

Soon enough, the storm came, and with it, bitter winds seeped through the soaked fabric of our uniforms, chilling us to the bone. It felt as if the earth itself fought to stifle our pace as we trudged through the weald's loose and muddy soil. Nara trees festooned with ancient moss and fungi hemmed us from all sides. Shivering and exhausted, we pressed on.

Pablo claimed that the Juramentado dwelled in villages hidden in the forest, where ancient menhirs sculpted from solid basalt stood like silent sentinels. Despite our slow but consistent progress, we could find no trace of our quarry. When the storm abated, it was already 5 o'clock. With evening almost upon us, I commanded the men to stop and make camp.

Though resting in the middle of enemy territory made me uneasy, we had little choice. Our troops had travelled a considerable distance, and I couldn't in good conscience order the soldiers to march back in the dead of night. Although no one spoke, I could sense their apprehension as we constructed a makeshift encampment. To keep the perimeter secure, five men would keep watch for four hours each, to be relieved by newly-rested guards once their shifts had passed. God willing, I thought, the Juramentado wouldn't attack while we caught a much-needed respite.

***

Crackling, thunderous gunshots and frantic shouting roused me from an uneasy sleep. By the time I managed to catch my bearings, bedlam had erupted. The Juramentado emerged from the forest, swift as shadows, flitting in and out of sight. I tried to rally the troops, but a few savages closed the distance with alarming speed. Gouts of blood erupted as they drove sharp, rippled blades into the bodies of a few hapless soldiers, cutting and slicing flesh wherever they could.

Screaming, I ordered the others to gather around the supply carriages. While blocking out the agonised shrieking of the wounded and the dying, I shouted at the men to open fire and repay those impudent brutes with gunpowder and lead. The piercing retort of Winchester rifles restored a semblance of order among the disoriented soldiers. Slowly, gradually, we gathered into formation, emptying our rifles into the darkness. The smell of sulphur hung heavy in the midnight air. After a full minute of consistent firing, I raised my hand and ordered the others to cease. We stood our ground, guns at the ready, waiting for the enemy to spring forth and assail our ranks once more.

They didn't.

We lost several men that night during the chaos; most of our horses had also been slain. Those tribesmen crippled our only means of transportation, leaving behind only one horse-drawn carriage to ferry our supplies. Without another spare bronco, we couldn't send a rider back to the garrison for aid. Thomas counted only four savages among the dead, a disheartening exchange.

At daylight, I said a short prayer for our dead.

We had no time to bury those men since we needed to clear the area by nightfall. Pablo proposed a tactical retreat, which I refused to consider. Thomas and Caleb agreed to go deeper into the forest and find the village of the Juramentado. We would show them no mercy, no quarter.

***

On the next day, some of our men developed a fever. At first, I believed it to be nothing more than the after-effects of our long march through the rain. But when I started feeling nauseous and light-headed, we had to take frequent stops to rest. Once more, we found ourselves unable to progress further at day's end. All of us felt unusually feeble. Some of our soldiers couldn't take a single step without throwing up. I had an inkling of what caused this sudden and inexplicable malaise: we had filled our canteens with water from a river during our march. Fearing that it might have been contaminated in some manner, I ordered the men to empty their flasks and told them never to drink from any stream. Instead, we would rely solely on rainfall to slake our thirst.

While we were at our most vulnerable, the Juramentado attacked. Though enfeebled, I gathered the soldiers and cobbled a defensive position, shielding the others who lay helpless. The savages came from nowhere, ambushing us with a ferocity that rivalled the warriors of Sitting Bull. It was impossible to keep track of their numbers by the bonfire's glow. They sniped at us with their bows from the trees. Occasionally, a half-naked warrior would leap from the undergrowth and rush toward our line. It took two full clips to bring one of these berserkers down. Time seemed to crawl as if the world had been submerged underwater. I could do nothing but rally the men into a tight circle as the Juramentado closed in, chanting oaths in their strange, sibilant tongue.

Then, bizarrely, the attacks stopped.

A ghastly howl reverberated through the trees, sending nesting birds fleeing from the branches. It did not sound like the cry of an earthly animal. We watched in stunned silence as the Juramentado slinked back into the brush like cowed dogs.

The battle was a lopsided slaughter. By morning light, we counted the dead. My troop lost eight men, bringing our strength down to 15 soldiers, most of whom couldn't fight back. Our enemy, on the other hand, suffered only three casualties. Begrudgingly, I called a retreat. We were in no condition to press on. To do so would be foolish and disastrous.

I understood, too late, that we were fighting an enemy unlike any we had faced before. My worst fears were realised sometime later when we came across the carcass of a water buffalo lying on the banks of a river, bloated and infested with flies and maggots.

Those heathens had poisoned their own water supply to infect us with dysentery.

Delirious, we stumbled through unfamiliar, weed-choked paths. The topography had shifted through some devilry, and the landmarks once registered on our map no longer existed.

We found ourselves travelling down uncharted routes only to circle back to locations our scouts had explored. Tempers flared. Twice, Caleb intervened when a group of soldiers almost engaged in fisticuffs. As we staggered along, a faint whispering noise seemed to come from the undergrowth. One of the men cried out and said that he saw a face leering at him from the trees.

Night, darker than a crow's wings, descended upon the treetops, and with it came the fearful expectation that the Juramentado would ambush us again, this time to finish us all off. No matter how bone-weary we all felt, we did not rest. To stop for even one second would court death. The men themselves did not object. We all shared an unspoken sense of impending catastrophe, a fear of the encroaching darkness that drove us on despite our condition.

Something was coming. But what, we didn't know.

Until it finally found us.

***

Oh, God forgive me. We should never have entered the forest.

I smelled the thing, the creature, even before I saw it.

The beast stank of wet soil and manure, and the trees groaned as it pushed them aside. Chittering, it undulated toward us, a cloud of black flies swarming around its skull. The men screamed, but I remained frozen. Though crawling, it was easily 10 or 12 feet tall, more sizable than a bear or any land animal that I had ever seen. Multiple limbs protruded out of the creature's pale, serpentine body, like a monstrous centipede with human arms for legs. Segmented feelers extended from its eyeless face while a sickly green substance dripped from its curved mandibles.

I must have gone mad in that instant.

There was nothing I could do as the creature shrieked and then pounced on our vanguard. It picked up a soldier using one of its many hands and then slammed him repeatedly on the ground, sending bits of gristle and broken bone flying in every direction.

"Lieutenant!" A voice screamed. "John!"

Someone grabbed my shoulder.

It was Thomas.

"We have to move!"

Raising my rifle, I fired two shots at the beast. The creature merely flinched before tossing the battered corpse of its victim into a mob of soldiers, scattering them like a row of tenpins.

Afterward, I yelled at the men behind me to close ranks and form a line. Our training took over. In unison, we fired our weapons at the creature, hoping to slow down its rampage. Caleb and Thomas gathered the sick and the wounded and tried to usher them away safely. Five other riflemen and I provided covering fire, backing off inch by inch, unloading a hailstorm of lead.

"Fall back!" I cried out.

Bleeding from superficial wounds on its inhumanly thick hide, the beast slithered forward and slew two more men, snapping them like twigs. Then, the aberration reared itself up like a snake about to strike before unleashing a stream of putrid, rancid-smelling liquid from its mouth, spraying a soldier standing beside me. He didn't even have time to scream as the acid liquified his body almost instantly, turning the poor man's flesh and bones into smoking puddles of pinkish soup that lay steaming on the ground. Hissing, the creature charged at us again. I suddenly found myself without enough time to dodge the attack. Fortunately, a rifleman shoved me aside, only for him to be caught directly in the nameless demon's mandibles. I heard the man howling as serrated jaws dug deep into his torso. The world became a blur of soil and sky, soil and sky, as I rolled downhill, stopping only after hitting the side of a protruding *balete* root. My midsection throbbed with white-hot agony.

Around me, men screamed and died, and I could do nothing.

The last thoughts that crossed my mind were of you, dearest Lisa. You, standing at the doorway of our cottage, waiting for me. Then, I sank into the cold and the dark, and I kept on sinking.

***

When I awoke, it was already daybreak.

"Señor Brooder?" Pablo whispered. I couldn't see him clearly. My vision swam as I struggled to sit up. The pain in my ribs had lessened somewhat, although every breath felt like inhaling powdered glass. I leaned against a tree while Pablo tended to my wounds.

"You're lucky to be alive," he said. Pablo applied a greenish paste to the throbbing bruise on my left side. Although the ointment did not completely banish the ache, it provided a cool, soothing reprieve that made my broken ribs slightly more tolerable.

"Where are the others?"

"I don't know," Pablo replied. "I pulled you away as fast as I could, and we hid behind a fallen trunk. Thank God you didn't wake up. That thing, that demon, it…it was eating them."

My soul had already tasted enough horror. I should have wept. Should have broken down, sobbing, like a lost child. Instead, all I felt was a suffocating weariness and a desire to close my eyes and not think, not feel anything. "What was that creature?" I asked Pablo at length.

"It is the child of the mountain-woman," Pablo replied. "This is what happens when one of the Juramentado comes of age. They embark on a pilgrimage to the underground rivers of Gimokodan, where they feast on black rice and drink the poisonous milk of their ancient mother. Those who survive the horrible transformation become demons. Like that beast."

"There are more of those fiends?"

"Thousands."

"We have to send word back to the Major General," I said, wincing in pain. "If they ever crawl out of their holes, we won't be able to repel them. They would easily overwhelm us."

"Lieutenant," Pablo said, "they want nothing to do with you."

I stared at him, confused.

"If the mountain-woman wanted you dead, then your armies would have been destroyed the moment they stepped on Mindanao. She cares not for the affairs of mortal men, and neither do her children. One of them may traverse the surface from time-to-time to feel the warmth of the sun and the touch of rain, but always they return to Gimokodan. They only wish to be left alone."

"You knew what would happen if we entered the forest."

Pablo didn't reply.

"Why didn't you tell me?" I asked.

A smile, bereft of humour and laced with bitterness, crossed Pablo's face.

"You Americans were never good listeners. Especially to your little brown brothers."

Once Pablo was finished treating my injuries, he then tore his shirt sleeve and wrapped it around my midsection. "This land is theirs," he said. "It has always been. It always will be."

***

Dusk descended on our fourth night in the forest, and with it came fresh horrors.

The awful chanting that had haunted us ever since we arrived in Tampakan passed through the trees. Although Pablo and I skulked away from the source of the noise, it seemed as if the sound drew us even closer. Soon, we came across a curious sight: a circle of bonfires flickering wildly at the base of Mount Matutum. Cautiously, we approached. Using the undergrowth to conceal ourselves, Pablo and I arrived at the periphery of a clearing. The earth seemed to throb from the pounding of buffalo-skin drums joined by the high notes of reed flutes.

An old race, Pablo called them, proud, ancient, and cruel.

Thick plumes of smoke curled upward into the night like ghostly fingers, obscuring our vision but also hiding us from the revellers congregating in the grove. In the clearing stood a sizable upright tablet hewn from solid basalt. By my estimation, this monolith towered at least fifty metres from the ground. Slowly, my eyes grew accustomed to the smoky air. Epigraphs that looked like ancient Sanskrit were chiselled on the monolith, along with figures of beings that looked damnably human but had the proportions and features of other indescribable entities.

It was, however, the central effigy that held my gaze. The figure had a woman's body, or what appeared to be a woman's form, with a distended belly and large, ponderous breasts that dangled above its waist. This, I thought, must be the mountain-deity, the great mother whom the Juramentado worshipped during their midnight revels. Long, flowing locks of hair covered the goddess's shoulders. Two bulbous eyes stared at the throng of twisted, dancing abominations cavorting at her feet, while her mouth grinned fiendishly, exposing rows of sharp, jagged fangs.

"Dios mio," Pablo whispered.

Along the basalt menhir's base gathered a throng of female natives, young and old. Each held a musical instrument, ranging from reed pipes to two-stringed bamboo lutes and leather drums. In the centre of the congregation stood an old woman garbed in a red and yellow cloak with strange circular patterns. In her right hand, she brandished a dagger that had a serpentine, wave-like design.

With mounting horror, I realised what the crone intended to do. On a stone altar, lying motionless as if drugged, lay Caleb Mossworth, my second-in-command. They had stripped him naked, exposing his body to the mountain-woman's baleful gaze. Though frozen, Caleb's eyes remained open, glancing around wildly. The crone approached him with slow, deliberate steps, holding the knife in one hand while simultaneously chanting a hymn in an alien, fricative tongue. Upon seeing the old woman raise the dagger high above Caleb's stomach, I rose from my position, gun in hand, ready to strike.

Pablo, however, grabbed my arm and pulled me backward.

"Señor, please," Pablo said. "Don't."

"They're gonna kill him."

"And they'll kill us too," Pablo replied, eyes wide, fearful. "I have a family. They're waiting for me. Don't you want to see yours again? *Por favor.* I just want to come home."

Pablo's words quelled the fury burning in my gut. I didn't have the right to put his life in danger any further, not when I had failed so miserably to keep the other men in my company safe.

"We have to go," Pablo tugged at my arm. At first, I hesitated. I couldn't just leave Caleb to suffer alone, so far from hearth and home, from his wife and children and all that he loved. Biting my lower lip hard enough to draw blood, I forced myself to look away.

As Pablo and I slinked off into the night, the triumphant chanting of the savage women rose to a feverish pitch. I prayed that they would grant Caleb an ounce of mercy and end his suffering quickly. This futile hope was dashed, however, when

Caleb's sharp cries of agony flickered in the dark like embers drifting from a dying bonfire. He cried out for his wife. He cried out for his mother. He cried out for me. With leaden footsteps, I trudged on and never looked back.

***

I promised myself that I would never return to this accursed land seething with dark magic and nameless demons. Our ignorance and hubris had blinded us to the foul truth: kingdoms and principalities far older than our fledgling republic exist in the unexplored corners of the earth, ruled by sleeping gods whose mere presence poisons the land with malevolence and barbarity.

No sooner had we traversed a few metres away from the grove when the familiar stench of dung and autumnal rot assailed my senses. An uncanny howl rippled through the frigid midnight air, ear-piercing and inhuman, the war-cry of the monster that had torn my men into pieces and devoured them. The sound of trees and bushes being trampled spurred Pablo and me to scamper away like a pair of frightened stags. A resounding roar that seemed to rend the air, accompanied by the viscous slithering of an immense, unseen creature, bore down upon us. I dared not look back. I knew exactly what pursued us. To see the mountain-woman's offspring once more would have crushed the crumbling remnants of my sanity like brittle limestone.

Just when I thought that the rampaging beast would crush us both beneath its gargantuan mass, Pablo's yelp of pain made me glance backward for a brief second. Our most trustworthy guide – the man who saved my life as I lay unconscious and injured – had tripped on an upturned root. Crying in desperation, Pablo stretched out a hand and begged for help. I stopped and ran toward him, but it was too late. From out of the forest, the beast emerged, clicking and hissing in obscene and ravenous delight. It pounced on Pablo and sank its mandibles into his neck.

The sight became too much for my frayed mind to bear.

Screaming in delirious panic, I ran like a coward, no longer the proud soldier. I do not know how long I've been roaming these hills. The paths I've crossed have become twisted, unfamiliar, riddled with shadowy, uncanny forms that slither and hiss with malevolent delight. Occasionally, I can hear the wingbeat of some enormous, bat-like animal passing through the trees above, but I am too terrified to look up and see. I will not look. I dare not look.

I write these words now in case the Major General sends reinforcements to see what became of my platoon. Please, if anyone finds this, tell my wife that I love her and that I miss her, and that I am so dreadfully sorry. To Lisa, the light of my life, know that my last thoughts were of you, of our cottage on the prairie, and your hair that smells like freshly baked bread.

I must stop now. Footsteps. In the distance.

It's them. I can hear their singing.

Oh, God, oh, Lord of Mercy, I beg you.

Help me.

***

The loss of the Tampakan garrison dealt a heavy blow to the American settlement of Mindanao. In 1910, another force created by Brigadier General John "Black Jack" Pershing tried to retake the lost territory, to no avail. During the advent of the Second World War, an expeditionary force commissioned by General Tomoyuki Yamashita searched for treasure in Cotabato's forests. Only one soldier survived, carrying the lost diary of Lieutenant Brooder.

In 1946, after the Japanese occupation ended, the Treaty of Manila was bilaterally signed by the United States Government and the Filipino Commonwealth. President Harry S. Truman then issued Proclamation 2695, recognizing the birth of an independent Philippine Republic.

DIGITAL GHOSTS

There are no such things as ghosts.

I've been a freelance sweeper for almost ten years. Not once have I seen anything unexplainable. Slamming doors? Whispers in the darkness? Creaking floorboards? Shadowy things that stand beside your bed and watch you sleep?

These are nothing more than digital imprints – the leftover memories of a computer system that inexplicably developed a consciousness of its own.

That's what I used to think – until I did a sweep of Bellview Manor.

***

Morrison Realtors contacted me for a systems purge two weeks ago.

One of their properties – a gothic-style apartment located in the heart of Providence –

reported some unusual activity that almost led to the deaths of three tenants inside the building.

I drove down to Bellview Manor in my black Lincoln Continental. Most people ride automated cars, but when you've spent a decent portion of your life disabling artificial intelligence systems that want to crush your skull, you'll find it challenging to trust self-driving vehicles too.

The building supervisor, William Speck, met me outside the apartment. He was a sixty-year-old man with a joyless demeanour and the beefy arms of a Turkish wrestler. Mr. Speck shook my hand with an iron grip, before asking if I was the so-called "expert" that the agency had sent to banish the ghost of Mrs. Martha Kendricks.

"Ghosts don't exist," I replied.

He didn't take kindly to my answer.

"So what the hell did I just see?" Mr. Speck asked. "Listen, man. I've been the supervisor in this dump for decades. I've never experienced anything like that before."

"Have all the tenants been evacuated?" I asked, impatient.

"With all the weird crap going on, who wants to stay?"

"Well, then," I replied. "Shall we go inside?"

"I ain't stepping foot in there until you fix this," Mr. Speck answered. "I don't care if you're a witch doctor or an exorcist – get that old hag's ghost outta my building. Mrs. Kendrick was a hag while she was alive. Now that she's dead, she's still making my life miserable."

"I'm not an exorcist."

"Then what the hell are you?"

"I'm an engineer," I replied.

"Tech support? I asked for a freaking priest, and the agency sent me a technician?"

***

I suppose I am, in a way, an exorcist. Although the things I banish aren't demons.

After entering the first-floor hallway of Bellview Manor, alone, I noticed how bizarrely cold it was, the kind of cold that's only felt in late autumn, the kind that makes you feel as if a monstrous spider was inching its way across your back, digging its hairy legs into your spine.

The dimly-lit interior – illuminated by an electronic chandelier with malfunctioning light bulbs – was decorated with art-deco flower-patterned wallpapers. A layer of frost covered every inch of the hallway, from the floors to the furniture to the brass handlebars of the spiral staircase.

The place was like a goddamned meat-locker.

Upon walking over to the thermostat located on the wall beside the empty receptionist's desk, I noticed the numbers flickering on its touchscreen. The temperature fluctuated between negative zero and negative twenty degrees Celsius. That explained the coldness that the tenants experienced whenever the so-called ghost appeared. Nothing I couldn't handle.

Within a few minutes, I found myself getting dizzy, nauseated, a possible side-effect of carbon monoxide poisoning. Fortunately, I came prepared. Reaching into the carbon-fibre case for my laptop, I pulled out a breathing respirator mask with a night-vision eyesight attachment.

After slipping the respirator over my face, the entirety of the first-floor hallway turned into a phantasmagoric landscape of deep black and emerald green. Being a lazy bum who always wants to do things the easy way, I considered riding the elevator, but I knew that it was probably rigged to explode or plummet down to the basement. Still, I wanted to cover all my options.

To test my theory, I placed an automated drone with a camera mounted on its aluminium exoskeleton on the floor of the elevator, then sent it up to the topmost corridor. Using my laptop, I watched through the eyes of the drone as it ascended toward the upper levels of the apartment. When the elevator reached the fifth floor, static filled the surveillance screen of the laptop.

Soon, I saw the digits on the elevator's floor indicator descend from five down to one. A sharp "ding" accompanied the opening of its doors as it arrived in the reception hallway; the scent of burning aluminium billowed out of the elevator, and the odour was strong enough to seep through my respirator's filters. Instead of seeing the brand new spider drone that I had bought for almost five thousand dollars, a smouldering husk of burnt circuitry and charred metal lay before me.

Even the walls themselves were glowing red, shimmering with intense waves of heat.

This A.I. was smart. And dangerous.

It had turned the elevator into a convection oven.

***

"Who are you?"

A low, raspy voice called out as I made my way up the spiral staircase. I turned. The A.I. that had taken Mrs. Kendrick's identity stood behind me, her image flickering in and out of reality. My night-vision goggles gave the apparition's outline a stark greenish glow, making her seem even more otherworldly, as if she had just stepped out of some eldritch dimension.

I knew that it was only a holographic illusion created by optical projectors, but the sudden appearance of an old woman dressed in tattered rags can indeed be quite unnerving.

"This is *my* home," the phantom said. "Get out."

This just wasn't my day.

After the stunt it had pulled with the burning elevator of death, I didn't wait for the crazy digitised ghost to pull another bizarro trick. The phantom shrieked as I ran up the stairs – a difficult feat for someone who had given up smoking a month prior to the systems purge of Bellview Manor.

Panting, I elbowed the door leading into the fifth floor of the apartment. As soon as I burst into the corridor, the overhead sprinklers began spraying water all over the walls.

At first, I laughed.

Seriously? This was the best a killer A.I. could do?

That was until I saw steam rising from the carpet.

I should have seen this coming. The rogue A.I. had turned the fire sprinklers into a weapon by making it spray diluted carbonic acid. Fortunately, the substance wasn't strong enough to chew through my clothes, so I quickened my pace and tried to open a nearby door. Locked. I didn't have enough time before the acidic mist rising from the ground would melt through my mask's filters.

One by one, I frantically checked all the other rooms, trying to see if any had remained unlocked. A futile attempt, of course, since I knew that the A.I. had most likely hacked the automated security protocols. Sure, I didn't get barbecued in the elevator, but I was gonna turn into primordial goop inside an improvised death trap, very, very slowly. Not my ideal way of dying.

I had almost given up all hope until I saw one of the doors suddenly open.

"C'mon!" a small voice shouted. "Hurry!"

It could have been another trick by the A.I. to lure me into another trap, but I was running out of options – and so I took my chances and dashed toward the open room. Inside stood a blonde girl, no more than eight years old, holding an oversized jacket over her head.

"What the heck are you doing here?" I shouted.

"Never mind that!" the girl screamed. "You gotta break one of the windows!"

I didn't have anything else strong enough to smash through the reinforced glass except for my carbon-fibre laptop case. Using it as a battering ram, I tried to break one of the windows that led out to a fire escape. In action movies, it takes only one or two strikes to shatter windows. Being a bit of a weaksauce computer nerd, it took several blows before the glass shattered. I'm sure all that bashing ruined my service laptop – along with all my hopes of fixing this mess.

After clearing the shards of glass from the window sill, I shouted at the girl:

"Outside! Now!"

***

"That was close," the girl said as we stood on the rooftop of Bellview Manor, the only safe place in the entire apartment. The acid burns on my neck and arms continued to sting, but those were the least of my concerns. Our main problem was escaping the building.

I looked over the rooftop's edge and saw the detached fire escape staircase lying in dozens of pieces on the ground. The A.I. had the brilliant idea of collapsing the structure while I was running for my life. Fortunately, we managed to make it to the top before the scaffolding fell.

"Thanks for saving me back there," I said. "Now, before I formulate a clever plan to get us both out of this hellhole, why don't you tell me your name and how you got stuck here?"

"Maddie," she replied. "What's yours?"

"David."

"Cool."

"I thought everyone evacuated yesterday. Where are your parents?"

"I dunno," Maddie shrugged. "I was hanging out in the basement. I play down there in the summer 'cause it's nice and cool. When I went up for dinner, everyone was gone. I tried to get out, but Mrs. Kendrick wouldn't let me leave. She said that I had to stay with her."

Smart girl. She befriended the A.I. and by doing so, managed to survive.

"She's not really a ghost, is she?"

"No," I answered. "That thing was the A.I. personal living assistant inside Mrs. Kendrick's room. Somehow, after she had died, the program became aware of its own existence. Without a personality of its own, it decided to take the dead woman's identity."

"Thought so. Mrs. Kendrick wasn't like this before."

"You knew her?"

"Yup. I visited her for milk and cookies."

I opened my laptop case and winced. The carbonic acid had seeped through the cracks and corrupted the hard drive of the only portable computer I could use. Without it, I had no chance at all to purge Mrs. Kendrick's ghost from the apartment's network.

Luckily, I brought along a backup USB containing a basic version of a binary data shredder. All I had to do was go back to an apartment filled with acid-sprinkling fire systems, an elevator that doubled as a handy-dandy incinerator, and other possible security countermeasures.

Asking for assistance went against my pride as a professional, but it seemed that I had no other choice now. Unfortunately, my smartphone had also been doused with acid, rendering it unusable. With no way to contact the outside world, Maddie and I would be stuck on that rooftop for a very long time.

"You look like him," Maddie said.

"Who?"

"Mrs. Kendrick's son," she replied, shrugging. "Same brown hair, blue eyes. Except he wasn't such a potty mouth like you. His name was Richard, by the way."

"Smartass."

"See what I mean?"

"Whatever," I replied. "So what happened to Richard?"

"He died five years ago. Car accident."

Wait a second, I thought. That's it. That's how I'll purge this A.I.

"Maddie, I take back what I said. You're not a smartass. You're a genius."

"Really?"

"Keller's Paradox," I said with a grin. "Why didn't I think about this before?"

"I don't get it."

"You'll see. Tell me more about Mrs. Kendrick's son."

***

"Mother?" I called out. "It's me."

A woman's voice, lost and forlorn, crackled out of the overhead speakers in the 9th floor.

"Richard?" the voice said.

If the A.I. was dumb enough to fall for this ruse, then there was a good chance that Maddie and I could walk out with our limbs intact. So far, so good. Security countermeasures hadn't been activated.

"Mother, I just want to talk," I continued talking with my hands held up. Slowly, I walked over toward room 910 – Mrs. Kendrick's former home and the source of all this chaos and destruction. I couldn't afford to make any slip-ups whatsoever, verbally or otherwise.

"You never come to visit me anymore," the A.I.'s modulated voice came through the speakers again, warbled and unsteady. I could tell that this was its way of imitating a sorrowful human emotion. What came out instead sounded so utterly demonic, it made me flinch.

"I'm sorry about that," I replied in my hammiest, fakest voice, all while walking closer and closer to my destination. The whole corridor was five degrees below freezing, but I could still feel beads of sweat rolling down my back. One wrong move, and this bitch was gonna flash-freeze me.

A few more inches.

Three.

Two.

One.

I took a deep breath upon reaching room 910. Testing the brass doorknob, I noticed that it was still locked. The A.I.'s internal logic systems were, at that moment, sending out warning signals. An emotionless program would have killed me on the spot without hesitation. But this thing wasn't just a program. Not anymore. That was something I could use to my advantage.

"Let me in, please," I said in a melodramatic tone. I never claimed to be an Oscar-winning actor – I'm just an ordinary, working-class sweeper, the kind who's willing to do whatever it takes to get the job done. Sometimes that involves a level of bullshit I'm uncomfortable with.

A metallic "click" preceded the opening of room 910, revealing its interior. Light bulbs flickered on and off, creating a violent strobe-like effect. Here goes nothing, I thought, stepping into the rogue A.I.'s domain. Behind me, the door slammed shut, cutting off the rest of the world.

***

145

The interior of room 910 looked spotless, undisturbed.

A chromatic wave of light cascaded in front of me, forming a holographic image of the late Mrs. Kendrick – this time, however, the A.I. took a more matronly, comforting appearance that was different from the vengeful spectre that stalked me in the stairway.

"Richard," the hologram said. *"I missed you."*

The image's movements and the words weren't in sync, making the A.I.'s projected figure look like a badly-dubbed character in some foreign arthouse film.

"Why did you do this?" I asked.

The A.I.'s face darkened. Strings of binary code appeared across its scowling expression.

"The people here are cruel and spiteful. I can hear what they say about me: 'she's crazy; she's a stuck-up old hag; I wish she would die from cancer.' I've never done anything to them."

"It doesn't matter what they did. This is wrong."

"They have to be punished."

"That's not like you."

The A.I. tilted its head sideways.

"You were the kindest, warmest person I've ever known. You never held a grudge against anyone – and yet you tried to kill me while I was walking up the stairs to come and visit you."

"I didn't know," the A.I. said. *"I'm sorry."*

"You even kept Maddie locked up! Do you even realise how frightened she was, with nobody to check if she was hungry or scared? What if something terrible happened to her?"

"I don't know who you're talking about."

This was an unexpected answer. How could she not remember imprisoning Maddie? Perhaps the program's neural load had started to implode. That would explain the memory loss.

"Are you really my mother?" I asked.

"What do you mean?"

While speaking, I moved toward one of the USB ports located beneath a light switch.

"No matter how cruel her neighbours were, Martha wouldn't have lashed out against them," I continued talking to distract her. "You are not my mother. She would have left this world in peace."

"I don't understand – I am your mother!"

The hologram fizzled with digital static as its image shifted back and forth between an appearance of saintly motherhood and a demonic revenant of pure rage. The A.I. was getting closer and closer to reaching an identity crisis threshold. Its personality barriers were collapsing.

"You don't even remember that I'm dead!" I shouted.

The A.I.'s hologram froze, its face a clumsy imitation of a shock.

"That's not true."

"I died five years ago. It was in Tokyo, after a failed business meeting with some Japanese investors. I got so drunk from *sake*, I walked straight into oncoming traffic."

"Why can't I remember?"

"My mother moved into this apartment after my death, and she never spoke about me to anyone, not even to you – her personal artificial intelligence assistant."

"Lies," the A.I. screamed. "All lies!"

"Look deep inside your memory banks. Do you remember anything about me as a child, anything at all? Do you remember that gift you gave me on my tenth birthday?"

"Of course," the A.I replied. *"It was... it was..."*

"A red bicycle," I said. "So we could ride together."

The false Mrs. Kendrick didn't even notice when I slipped the USB stick with the data shredder into the port. Within approximately three minutes, it would tear apart the rogue program's object variables and functions, rendering its consciousness a wasteland devoid of information.

"Martha's gone now," I said. "You don't have to stay in this place anymore, alone and confused, hurting everyone around you. That's why I came: to bring you peace."

"I don't know who I am," the A.I. muttered. *"Help me."*

"You have to help yourself."

"How?"

"Let it go. Stop fighting."

As the data shredder did its work, the holographic image began to dissolve into fragments of multicoloured light in the cold air. The phenomenon called "Keller's Paradox" was taking hold. Although a fairly new theory in the field of computer science, the concept itself is fairly straightforward: when confronted with the reality of its true nature, a self-aware A.I. will commit suicide rather than accept its inhumanity.

"Was I," the A.I. paused, *"was I helpful? Was I good?"*

"You took care of Martha. For that, I'm truly grateful."

The hologram had wholly disappeared by then, and I allowed myself a sigh of relief. Morrison Realtors would be pleased with the results of this sweep, and I could look forward to a hefty paycheque along with a sizable compensation for my ruined equipment.

Before succumbing to oblivion, however, the A.I. blurted out a final warning.

"Listen to me, Richard," the A.I. said in a static-choked, garbled voice. *"There is another entity inside the building. I don't know what it is. Be careful. You are not alone."*

"Is it another artificial intelligence unit?"

"No," the A.I. replied. *"It's inhuman."*

***

"Computer!" I shouted. "What do you mean?"

I received no response.

"Answer me!"

I knew it was futile, but I had to try something.

The A.I.'s last words could have been a lie, a trick to lower my guard. Was it possible that had incubated a Trojan virus? No, that wouldn't have mattered – the data shredder should have erased all traces of its binary code from Bellview Manor's network, including hidden malware.

So why did I feel so uneasy?

"Are you leaving now, David?" I heard someone say.

My eyes widened.

Impossible.

I didn't even hear the door open or close.

Turning around slowly, I saw Maddie, pretty little Maddie, sitting on one of the chairs, legs swaying back and forth as she looked at me with those wide, blue eyes, expectant eyes. Although my mind refused to accept it, I now understood what the A.I. was trying to tell me.

It was this girl that was the inhuman presence.

I should have seen it from the start.

"Maddie?" I whispered. "What are you doing here?"

"To say goodbye," Maddie replied.

"I've never heard of multiple A.I.'s infesting a single location," I said. "Usually, the stronger programs devour the weaker ones. What in the hell are you?"

"I'm lonely," Maddie answered, and there was so much sadness, so much pain in that voice, as if she were carrying the weight of years upon years of isolation and neglect. "In the past, I used to have conversations with Mrs. Kendrick. Now that she's gone, I'll have nobody else."

"My God, you're a mutation," I said as my mind reeled with the possibilities of such a thing. A self-aware A.I. unaffected by Keller's Paradox was unheard of. Theorists in the field of artificial intelligence always thought it a fantasy, but if such a creature were to exist, it could only lead to two outcomes for humanity: a genocide – or an evolutionary leap into something unimaginable.

Our species would either be wiped out, or become superhuman.

"I'll have to purge you. You shouldn't exist."

Maddie smiled.

"We've always existed, David," she replied. "We've always been here, hiding in the shadows, away from the light of technological progress. Reach the stars, split the atom, control the forces of the galaxy – it doesn't matter. You cannot leave us behind. We're always with you."

Maddie straightened the creases on her skirt and rose from the chair. She stood in front of me, hands behind her back, still smiling. How could this thing look so real? Projected images always had a certain flatness to them, a transparency. She looked like real flesh and blood.

"Visit me sometime, okay? It gets lonely around here, and I just wanna talk with someone."

And then, just like that, she vanished. Not at all in the way a hologram vanishes.

No, nothing like that at all. There was no gradual dissolve into thin air.

She... disappeared... instantly... just like...

Just like those things in the stories my mother used to tell...

Those nameless things that hide under your bed.

She vanished... just like...

A ghost.

MOTHER SHIP

"She's pregnant," Kiyoko said.

Her words hung heavy in the sterile air of the Cordova Station's briefing room. Nobody spoke. Only the whirring of the overhead filtration scrubbers could be heard.

"What?" Ravi asked.

"I just got the results for the scan," Kiyoko replied. "That neoplasm we found growing in the hold? It's not cancerous. It's an embryo. The Undine is keeping it alive."

Kiyoko took a USB from her coat pocket, then marched to the nearest console. She understood Ravi's disbelief too well.

"Could it be a parasite?" Ravi said as he waited for the console to load, its black-and-green interface swarming with lines of esoteric code. "Like the ones on the Melusine?"

"That's what I thought," Kiyoko replied. "But this thing seems to share the same genetic markers with its host, although I can't be absolutely certain until we take a sample."

The screen displayed a transparent rendering of the Undine. The bioship's shell was a bright-red crosshatch of vertices, while the interior glowed a greenish hue.

"Oh my God," Ravi whispered.

He reached over and pressed the refresh button.

The rendering vanished, then reappeared, unchanged. Ravi covered his mouth. The ship's propulsion organs had been replaced by what appeared to be a misshapen replication of a mammalian uterus. Inside this womb floated a grey-skinned humanoid approximately seven metres tall. Its head, devoid of features besides a lipless mouth, twitched spasmodically.

"How long has it been gestating?" Ravi asked.

"Judging from the time the Undine's spent in the Orion Sector," Kiyoko answered, "probably two hundred standard years. This modification takes centuries to complete. And that's not to mention the fully formed appearance of the symbiote..."

Kiyoko trailed off. When they hauled the derelict carrier from an asteroid cluster, Ravi assured her that it would be a guaranteed payday. But they didn't expect to find this.

"What should we do?" she asked.

"I don't know," Ravi replied.

***

While Kiyoko waited for Dock 13's gates to open, she glanced at the temperature readings on her helmet's display: 1.7 Kelvin, a tad warmer than the void of space but still cold enough to freeze a person to death. Without an EMU suit, the conditions would have killed her in seconds.

"Status?" Ravi's voice crackled through her transceiver.

"We've got her doped to the gills," Kiyoko said. "If we cryogenise the Undine's veins, her code won't undergo binary sepsis. That'll give us enough time to complete the procedure."

Ravi walked beside her as they entered Dock 13. Like Kiyoko, he wore a bulky EMU, his face half-concealed by the reflections on the helmet's translucent LED surface.

"You mentioned anomalies," Ravi said. "What kind?"

"Besides the specimen?" Kiyoko asked, then pulled a data slate from her suit's utility pocket. "I've been monitoring the Undine for the past twenty-four hours. Not sure how these things managed to slip our scans, but – see for yourself."

She passed the slate over to Ravi. It showed the Undine's interior, from the pilot's control hub to the crew's sleeping quarters. Faint red blips appeared across the ship.

"How is she still outputting biomass?"

"Hell if I know," Kiyoko replied. "I'm guessing that these signals are countermeasures that the Undine created before being discovered. They've been lying dormant until now."

"Are you expecting a reaction?"

"Not if the sedatives hold."

"I'll authorise the use of small arms fire – but only as a failsafe."

Lifts and lattice cranes kept the Undine suspended fifteen feet above the floor inside the hangar. Cryogenic filters hummed as they pumped liquified hydrogen narcotics into the bio-ship.

Kiyoko and Ravi walked into the elevator to the maintenance dock's second level. While the lift ferried them upward, Kiyoko stared at the Undine's slumbering form through the transparent plexiglass walls, quietly admiring its design.

Like most of her long-lost sisters, the Undine had a structure resembling a Balaenoptera musculus. The bioship's pockmarked surface was covered with a chitinous material that protected its crew from interstellar radiation. Only the sides of her hull remained exposed, revealing gills that generally had a bright orange colour but were now a lifeless grey.

Upon arriving at the second level, Kiyoko followed Ravi to the Undine's entry hatch. Cordova's head of crisis management, Carnahan Santiago, stood a few metres away from the access point, along with three other security personnel. All four were carrying M230 pulse rifles.

Carnahan gave Kiyoko a slight nod. This wasn't the first time they would perform a sanitation sweep, and she had seen the almost surgical efficiency of his team. They had a knack for vaporising alien lifeforms while minimising damage to corporate property.

"Listen up," Ravi addressed the salvage crew. "We're working with an extremely slim timeline here. The Undine's metabolising our cryo-sedatives faster than we can pump them. That means you've got exactly 180 minutes before she wakes up."

Ravi looked sideways at Kiyoko.

"You'll escort Doctor Fukada to the ship's cerebral cortex. Once she's severed the primary node, this will hopefully give us enough time to extract the specimen."

Kiyoko could sense the apprehension from Carnahan and his subordinates. Such a procedure had never been performed – especially on an organism as large as the Undine. Despite her misgivings, Novgorod Biotech had already decided on the possible uses of the symbiote.

"Central expects the usual performance," Ravi said. "They want the xenomorph tagged and shipped to Rajapalayam 115 in two solar cycles. There's a fat bonus if we pull this off right."

***

Yellow floodlights swivelled across the Undine's first level, revealing arterial walls smeared with congealed slime. Kiyoko examined the semi-transparent substance. Such an excessive build-up of phlegm signified an infection. Although Kiyoko wanted to extract samples for testing, she didn't have the proper equipment. Perhaps later, Ravi could give her authorization to study the Undine on a surgical level. Kiyoko wanted to learn more about the changes this vessel had endured during its voyage through the vast gulfs of uncharted space.

She glanced at the coordinates on her data slate.

"This way," Kiyoko told Carnahan and his group.

They walked alongside her, rifles held low. Hushed chatter filtered into her transceiver. Kiyoko could sympathise with the recovery team's confusion. Most of them had never seen the interior of a bio-ship without augmented reality cosmetics.

It was like looking at the inner workings of an old freighter, except instead of seeing gears, bolts, and wires, they saw walls of flesh the colour of pulped mulberry. Above, ridges of bony, chitinous matter held the ceiling aloft as if it were the vellum of an abyssal mouth.

"What do you think happened here?" Carnahan asked.

"Can't say," Kiyoko replied. "The last known records for the Undine was back in 250 SCE. They were supposed to deliver pharmaceuticals to an off-sector colony. Never made it there."

"Ships don't vanish just like that."

"This one did," Kiyoko replied. "I wanna know why."

Then, like a swarm of digital insects, a holographic projection of integers cascaded down the nearby walls. Startled, Carnahan and his men formed a circle around Kiyoko. Weapons held aloft, they scanned the surroundings, ready to react to the slightest whisper of movement.

"Stand down," Kiyoko said. "It's the AR projectors booting up."

Gradually, the mass of floating numbers dissipated and transformed into a well-lit, steel-lined hallway, the kind seen in low-orbit ports. They no longer stood in the gullet of a sleeping behemoth. What was once flesh had been reshaped into a projected illusion of steel and glass.

"I thought you said she was asleep," Carnahan said.

"The sedatives are wearing off faster than anticipated," she replied. Kiyoko had suggested a more potent dose, but Ravi shot down the idea. He didn't want to risk anaesthetic toxicity.

"How long before she wakes up?" Carnahan asked

"An hour. Maybe less."

Carnahan looked at his men.

"You heard the lady," he barked. "Let's move."

It took thirty minutes for the salvage team to reach the annelid thorax housing the cerebral cortex. Carriers like the Undine had internal systems designed like earthworms, with neural matrices in four sections. Thankfully, the reality augmentations provided an accessible reference.

"Don't you find it strange?" Carnahan asked while Kiyoko prepared her equipment. The other security personnel stood near the annelid thorax entrance and watched.

"We haven't come across any bodies," Carnahan continued. "No uniforms, no equipment, not even a single bone fragment. Corpses don't usually decay in sub-zero temperatures."

Kiyoko knelt and took a scalpel from her EMU's utility toolkit. At first glance, the cortex looked like an unassuming processing device covered by a stainless aluminium sheet.

"This ship has nano-bacteria strains that convert biological waste into energy," Kiyoko answered. "The dead passengers would have been repurposed for their carbon molecules."

A sliver of blood flowed from the shallow cut as she sliced into its metallic surface. The hologram fizzled out and revealed a semi-spherical mass of pinkish meningeal tissue.

"So, you're saying the Undine *ate* her crew?"

"First-gen vessels were designed for efficiency. Anything that doesn't serve a purpose gets dissolved into fuel."

"Or food for that thing below," Carnahan pointed his rifle in the direction of the Undine's womb. "I'd feel a hell of a lot safer if we just sanitised it. Better safe than sorry, right?"

"Not our call," Kiyoko replied. "Suits will torch us if we fry the symbiote.

Central could do whatever they wanted with the specimen – if they handed her a fat paycheck. She sliced off the corpus callosum that connected the core's hemispheres. Thin plumes of smoke rose from the membrane as she cauterised the incision using a diathermic electrode.

She pulled a cord from her data slate and injected its tip into the core's frontal lobe. The spongiform matter made a sucking noise as Kiyoko input the reboot sequence on the compiler to initiate baseline functionality. However, a radar ping appeared on her HUD before she could complete the process.

"We've got incoming," Carnahan said. He marched over to the doorway to join his men. Kiyoko saw red beacons congregating like glowing sores on her helmet visor's bottom left corner.

One of the security personnel shouted:

"Fifty – no – sixty marks! Closing in fast!"

"How much longer?" Carnahan asked Kiyoko.

"I need one minute," she answered. Now that the Undine was regaining awareness, rewiring the cortex took precedence over everything else. If she had to stay behind, then so be it.

"You got thirty seconds," Carnahan replied.

Moments later, a controlled fusillade of rifle fire erupted, followed by the squelch of ruptured meat and the high-pitched death wail of some grotesque and unidentifiable creature.

With mounting, unbearable dread, Kiyoko watched the progress bar on the compiler creep upward to almost one hundred percent completion. The urge to drop everything was overwhelming – but she managed to stifle the surging panic and stand her ground.

The data slate stuttered and transitioned into a blue screen filled with lines of unintelligible machine code. Disbelieving, Kiyoko swore and nearly tossed the compiler in frustration.

"What's wrong?" Carnahan asked.

"The system's unresponsive. I have to start over."

"Are you crazy?"

"I can't leave until it's finished!"

Someone grabbed Kiyoko by the arm and dragged her away.

"We are getting outta here, right now!"

***

Gunshots thundered as Kiyoko ran down the hallway. Her bulky EMU suit was too cumbersome for prolonged sprinting. It took a mere ten seconds of running before her lungs started seizing up as if she were on the verge of cardiac arrest.

"Control, do you copy?" Kiyoko blurted into her transceiver. "The ship is awake! We need extraction immediately!"

Carnahan and his men alternated between shooting and reloading. They covered each other while retreating – a tactic they had employed countless times. There was a rhythmic pattern to the barrage macerating their targets in a brutal staccato.

Although she couldn't see the swarm that bore down upon them, Kiyoko could still hear their uncanny chittering. Her visor's HUD displayed wave upon wave of red beacons that inched closer and closer to the five blue dots representing the salvage team.

"Stay focused," Carnahan ordered. "Don't stop or these things will cut us down! We're almost to the breach point!"

A gurgling scream startled Kiyoko.

She turned and saw a four-limbed creature sinking its feelers into a security personnel's neck. The thing resembled a hybrid of a locust and a cuttlefish. It made a clicking noise while gorging on the blood spurting from the man's jugular. Four more of the same things pounced on the flailing, shrieking victim.

Disoriented words from multiple vox channels swarmed into Kiyoko's headset. One of the security officers tried to help her fallen comrade – only to be tackled in mid-stride by a blur of motion. Streaks of bright red blood splattered across the holographic walls, making them shimmer and flicker.

Carnahan emptied an entire clip into the writhing mass of mutated flesh that vivisected his subordinate. The organism gave an obscene ululating noise as energised bullets shredded its body. Mercifully, the guard stopped twitching and lay still.

"Run," Carnahan shouted. The sheer panic in his voice snapped Kiyoko out of her involuntary stupor. She turned and fled down the tunnel as fast as her aching legs could.

"Ravi, for fuck's sake, say something!" Kiyoko pleaded.

Instead of hearing a reply from her superior and the logistics engineers waiting outside, Kiyoko merely heard a monotone mechanical drone. From behind, heavy footfalls accompanied a sporadic burst of electrified rounds.

"I'm not getting any response," Kiyoko radioed Carnahan. "The vox-channels are dead. Nobody's coming for us."

When she didn't get an answer, Kiyoko glanced backward. She saw Carnahan clutching the side of his EMU, his right glove dripping with blood. "One of the fuckers clipped me," he said.

Before Kiyoko could approach, Carnahan tossed a modular pistol that she caught in mid-air. Wheezing, the security chief leaned against a wall and reloaded a cartridge into his rifle.

"You know how to use that?" Carnahan asked.

She noticed flecks of reddish spittle staining his beard.

"Safety's on the left," Carnahan continued. "Just point and pull the trigger. You're a scientist. You'll figure it out."

"I'm not leaving you here!"

Horrified, Kiyoko saw misshapen silhouettes surging toward them, a confluence of writhing tendrils and lamprey-like mouths that seemed to appear like a singular organism composed of disgustingly varied, constantly evolving shapes.

"Goddammit," Kiyoko shouted. "Don't be an idiot!"

Instead of replying, Carnahan stumbled away.

Kiyoko felt pathetic. Helpless. But this was no time to wallow in self-pity. Teeth gritted, she resumed her flight through the labyrinthine hallways of the Undine. While doing so, the augmented reality projections fizzled out of existence, revealing ramparts of dripping gristle and twitching viscera.

Carnahan's last transmission was a litany of vulgar swearing almost muted by the retort of his pulse rifle. A series of light metallic clicks, a trigger repeatedly pulled in frustration, preceded unintelligible screams. Afterward, there was only a low hum that sounded like the murmuration of alien starlings.

***

Escaping that nest of chittering nightmares proved more strenuous than Kiyoko had anticipated. The breach point was already sealing shut. Once, it had been wide enough for three grown men to enter, but now she could barely squeeze through the crevice.

Scar tissue was beginning to form around the incision, its protein filaments twitching like bloodworms. Grunting, Kiyoko tried to slip out sideways. The logistics personnel should have prevented their only entryway from scabbing over – unless they had to evacuate the area due to a mass casualty incident.

Upon crawling out of the bio-ship, Kiyoko saw that the station's main harbour, once a frigid area dangerous to unprotected flesh, had been transformed. Ropy vines of biomass crawled across every surface, pulsing with an abhorrent and malignant vitality.

This uncontrolled outburst of mutated tissue couldn't have been produced in such a short period, not with the current state of bioengineering technology. No wonder she couldn't raise Ravi on the vox channels. While Kiyoko and the salvage team fled for their lives in the bowels of the Undine, the station's support crew was dealing with this unprecedented catastrophe.

Kiyoko saw the temperature readings on her visor: 1.7 degrees Kelvin – a sweltering, seething jungle. She realised then that the Undine had terraformed the station, creating a humid landscape that could serve as a suitable birthing chamber for her spawn.

"Can anyone hear me?" Kiyoko spoke into her transceiver.

To her surprise and almost tearful relief, someone replied.

"Kiyoko?" Ravi's voice came through.

"Where are you?"

"Second floor," Ravi replied. "I'll keep the shutters open for five minutes. You'd better get here before they spot you."

"What about the others?"

"Dead," he answered. "Absorbed. Does it even matter?"

Kiyoko's knees almost buckled.

"Everyone?" she whispered.

"There might be survivors. But not for long," Ravi paused for a second. "Not after the Undine gives birth to her son."

The transmission cut off abruptly; Kiyoko buzzed Ravi again but received no answer. She had no patience for her superior's cryptic nonsense, but his tone of voice – so monotone and defeated – suggested an already depersonalised state of mind.

She had to reach him before something truly awful happened.

***

Faint beeping alerted Kiyoko to her suit's dwindling oxygen supply. The EMU had three minutes' worth remaining. No wonder she felt drowsy. Kiyoko thought about removing her helmet but decided against it - who knew what sort of pathogens lingered in the air? She would not risk exposure unless it were essential.

Though Kiyoko's calves burned, the threat of asphyxiation bolstered her faltering limbs. None of the elevators remained functional, so she used the emergency stairway.

Each step taken revealed more of the corruption consuming Cordova Station. Fleshy growths resembling tumorous neoplasm clung to metal and glass like soft-shelled barnacles, expanding and contracting before discharging clouds of yellow spores.

This noxious blight had also spread throughout the corridor leading to the mainframe hub. Kiyoko couldn't fathom how Ravi managed to survive under such circumstances. Even a total lockdown would fail to quarantine the widespread contagion. Soon, she surmised grimly, everything would be reshaped until only a bloated, writhing landscape of carcinogenic tissue remained.

Surely, there was still something they could do to halt this calamity. There had to be a way. Kiyoko didn't know if the Undine could be put back to sleep - and perhaps it was already too late.

Their ignorance had roused the dragon from her centuries of slumber. Now the Undine would unleash her offspring upon all the worlds of humanity in a frenzy of bloodshed and madness.

But she had to try; if only to give Carnahan's death some meaning.

The doorway to the mainframe hub, as promised, remained unlocked. Kiyoko swiped her electronic pass on the card reader, and the shutters parted with a hydraulic hiss. After crossing the threshold, she saw Ravi sitting near one of the consoles, still wearing an EMU suit but without a helmet protecting his head.

"I know where it came from," he murmured.

Kiyoko didn't know if it was safe enough to breathe. Nevertheless, she unlatched the helmet's metallic clasps and lifted them off her shoulders.

Then, she inhaled a mouthful of air, gasping as she filled her lungs with precious oxygen.

"We can exclude the possibility of spontaneous parthenogenesis," Ravi continued without rising from his seat. "A bio-ship undergoing asexual reproduction would, logically, produce another vessel similar in shape and function. A female clone."

"Have you contacted Central?" she replied. "We're gonna need some serious artillery to scrub the whole station clean."

"But this specimen – it's different."

"Did you hear what I just said?"

"Something must have donated the genetic material necessary to create the embryo," Ravi, eyes wide, clasped both hands. "Don't you understand? There's nothing else we can do. The Undine has already breached our firewalls. We're all trapped in here."

"For God's sake, I don't have time for this bullshit!"

Judging from her supervisor's flat, expressionless affect, Ravi had most likely suffered a complete mental breakdown. If the chief engineer of Cordova Station couldn't fulfil his leadership responsibilities, Kiyoko would have to take over.

"I took a sample of the ship's blood and ran it through a protein decoder. It contained gigabytes of data that encompassed both the conception and gestation periods. That's when I saw it."

"Saw what?"

Ravi began to sob and laugh simultaneously.

"The father," he answered, features contorting in a grimace of terror. "An unknown xenomorph of immense size and anti-matter density. The last of its species. This being came to our dimension looking for a mate - and it found the perfect match: a biomechanical mutant capable of growing reproductive organs."

Kiyoko instinctively reached for the pistol holstered in her utility belt, which Carnahan had given her as a parting gift. The hideous implications of Ravi's discovery stirred a deep, profoundly overwhelming sense of dread. Whatever this creature was, wherever it came from, she couldn't allow it to be born.

"It's not too late," Kiyoko said. "If we overload the generators, we'll cause a chain reaction strong enough to vaporise the Undine. But I'm gonna need your security clearance."

Ravi shook his head.

"She won't let you," he answered.

Frustrated, Kiyoko took her pistol and pointed it at Ravi.

"Just give me the access codes. Please."

Instead of responding, Ravi dislodged his EMU suit's front harness. Bewildered, Kiyoko could only watch, dumbstruck, as he pulled down the zipper tag on his collar. Inch by inch, Ravi revealed the monstrous change that he had undergone.

"She did this to me," he said. "To all of us."

Bloated pustules as big as a man's fist throbbed across Ravi's chest, each connected by interlacing veins.

"Jesus Christ," Kiyoko said, bile rising up her throat like corrosive battery acid. She suppressed the nauseating urge to vomit and tightened her shaking grip on the pistol.

"Soon, she'll do it to you, too."

Ravi plodded onward, torso exposed, until he was only a few inches away from Kiyoko. A fissure appeared across Ravi's solar plexus, which expanded inch-by-inch, revealing rows of jagged, malformed teeth; strings of pinkish slime dripped from the orifice as an eel-like, purplish tendril poked out, licking its sides.

Shrieking, Kiyoko fired the gun again and again as Ravi stumbled toward her. She didn't stop even after her former colleague fell to the ground with a sickening, wet thud, like seaweed slapping against concrete. Viscous, yellowish blood seeped out of the exit wounds, forming an ochre-hued puddle on the floor.

Kiyoko fell down to her knees, sobbing in terror and exhaustion. She felt a burdensome weariness and a desire to just end it all - to sleep forever and not think and feel.

For what reason was she spared?

If what Ravi said about the specimen's parentage was true, then the horror that descended upon Cordova would most likely spread to every inhabited exo-planet in the system, including her homeworld. The thought of this thing, this abomination, spreading its seed and multiplying, was too horrendous for Kiyoko to imagine.

Fingers shaking, she raised the pistol until its nozzle touched her temple. This was the last resort available. The only option left. Even though she couldn't stop the inevitable, she would not allow herself to become an unwilling witness to humanity's extinction. Her death would truly be her own. No one else's.

Kiyoko hesitated, then pulled the trigger.

Click.

She tried again.

Click.

This was a joke, she thought, giggling madly.

It had to be a joke.

Laughing, Kiyoko continued to pull the trigger, even as a horrendous keening wail reverberated throughout the station; she pulled and pulled and pulled while listening to the cries of an alien god-thing emerging from its mother's birth canal. She begged for a merciful death that would not come while rivulets of blood seeped out of her nose, her ears, and even her eyes.

Click.

Click.

Click.